THE NIGH...

FINNEGAN

QUICK

THE NIGHTMARES OF FINNEGAN QUICK

LARRY HAYES

BLOOMSBURY
CHILDREN'S BOOKS
LONDON OXFORD NEW YORK NEW DELHI SYDNEY

BLOOMSBURY CHILDREN'S BOOKS
Bloomsbury Publishing Plc
50 Bedford Square, London WC1B 3DP, UK
29 Earlsfort Terrace, Dublin 2, Ireland

BLOOMSBURY, BLOOMSBURY CHILDREN'S BOOKS and the Diana logo
are trademarks of Bloomsbury Publishing Plc

First published in Great Britain in 2025 by Bloomsbury Publishing Plc

A catalogue record for this book is available from the British Library

ISBN: PB: 978-1-5266-7778-5; eBook: 978-1-5266-7777-8;
ePDF: 978-1-5266-8543-8

2 4 6 8 10 9 7 5 3 1

Typeset by RefineCatch Limited, Bungay, Suffolk

Printed and bound in Great Britain by CPI Group (UK) Ltd, Croydon CR0 4YY

MIX
Paper | Supporting
responsible forestry
FSC® C171272

To find out more about our authors and books visit www.bloomsbury.com
and sign up for our newsletters

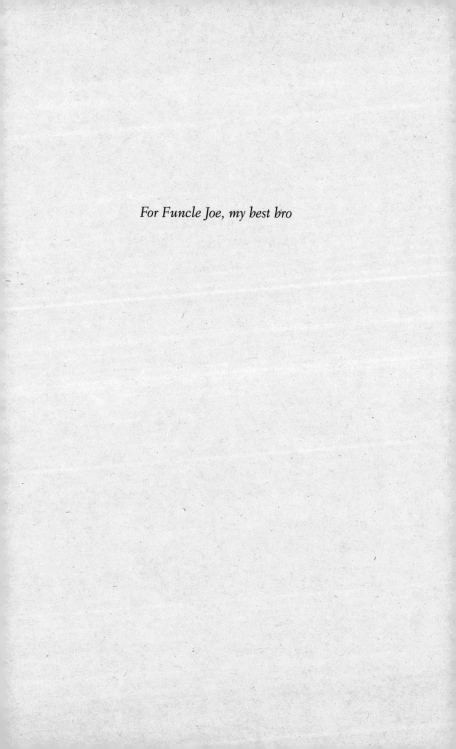

For Funcle Joe, my best bro

FRIDAY, 9TH SEPTEMBER

Whoever finds this, be warned. This is going to creep you out. And it's going to get creepy, fast. So if you're someone who talks tough but still needs a light on when you go to bed – just stop reading. Do yourself a favour and read something else. I'm not judging you. I go to sleep with *all* the lights on. You will too when you know what I know.

Because what I'm going to tell you will change *everything*. Once you know what's out there, and what they want, the world won't ever be the same again.

You know the stuff we're all afraid of? The things they make horror movies and write books about? Vampires and werewolves and zombies and devils and demons and creepy little kids on tricycles who suck out your

1

soul? Well, we're scared of them for a reason.

We fear them because we've *seen* them. Because they exist. And they come for us every time we sleep. They come for all of us. And the only reason they haven't got you yet – well, it's because of people like me. People who go to sleep every night with their arm in a bucket of warm water.

But I'll get to all that later, because I've got the whole night to write this. It's not like I'm going to sleep, not tonight of all nights. So I might as well start at the beginning and tell you everything. And if by some freak disaster I do fall asleep, at least someone will know the truth. Because frankly, at this precise moment in time, I'm the only one left who knows what's happened.

They've already got my shadow – the one they replaced it with is pretty gross. And once they get the rest of me, this notebook will be all there is. The only evidence that I or my family ever even existed.

You see, that's how it works. The monsters, in my dreams, are always hunting. Hunting me. They come in all shapes and sizes. Some are animals, some human. And some, you couldn't make up – zombies with melted faces and vampires starting to rot. But there's one monster, a woman, who is always there when something really, truly terrible happens. She lurks on the edges of dreams waiting to snatch things. And by things – I mean my family.

My dog was first, eight years ago, when I, Finnegan Quick, was just a little scrat. It's my first ever memory, so we may as well start there.

1

MY FIRST MEMORY

I was young, not even at school, and we had a dog, a white terrier called Biscuit. But then I started having dreams about him.

There'd be a knock on the front door, a big, heavy knock, like a knock of doom. I'd be sitting on the kitchen floor doing a jigsaw or whatever four-year-olds do and I'd hear that big old, heavy knock on the front door. Like it was done with a massive fist. Biscuit would go nuts – running about, barking, growling, but no one else would even notice. Mum and Dad just carried on, like they hadn't heard a thing. That's when I'd know it was a dream and not real, because no one could have ignored that knock, not in real life. I'd wake up then, screaming my little toddler lungs out.

And that's how it went on – for weeks, maybe even months. But then the dream started changing. *Growing*. The first bit was just like before, except now the door would open. I'd look through from the kitchen into the hallway and I'd see a shadow on the wooden floor. And then a hand would reach into the hallway, to pet Biscuit.

It was a woman's hand but deathly white, empty of blood. And all the creepier because the nails were bright crimson. They were long and pointed, and as the hand reached down to pat Biscuit, blood would drip on to his trembling head.

'There's a good doggie,' she would say. But in a rasping, grating voice that seemed somehow less than human.

I always shut my eyes then. Boy, did I shut my eyes, because I knew that, whoever she was, if I opened my eyes – if that woman looked into my eyes – *she'd get me*.

And every night the dream story grew.

With my eyes shut, I never saw what happened next. But I heard it. And I *smelt* it. Whatever the creature was, it came into our house smelling of death. Like raw meat left in a bin.

And the sounds: I'd hear our little Biscuit, growling, then biting and barking and fighting with the fury of pure, utter terror.

Until one night when I dreamed my dream, the barking stopped. I opened my eyes to see Biscuit lying on the floor, eyes open, breathing stopped, as that hand dragged him out the front door.

But that's not the freaky thing. That's not *the secret*. The secret that's been haunting me all these years is that my dreams don't just stay in my head. They change the world. They leave wounds and scars.

Because the next morning, when we went down for breakfast, Biscuit was gone. And not just him. His bed was gone too, and the dog bowl, chews, everything. Mum and Dad didn't say a word. No one said a word. It was like he'd never, ever even existed.

Told you this was going to get creepy. But it's nothing compared to what happened next.

2

WHAT HAPPENED NEXT

People say that if you die in a dream, you die in real life. They also say that if you wee in a dream, you wet yourself in real life. But that's not true either, not for most people. Try it if you don't believe me. People, pretty much, don't know what they're talking about.

But me? I'm different. If you wee yourself in my dreams, the bed gets wet. And if you die in my dreams, well, being dead in real life is the least of it. You don't *just* die for real.

It's much, much worse than that.

I know because I've seen it happen. About a year after our dog died, just after I started school, they took Mum.

It started with a new dream about the woman, this

time in the play park. And like before, I never got a proper look at her. I just knew she was there – talking to my mum on the park bench while I played in the sand, too afraid to look round. Terrified of what I might see, knowing that my mum would soon start screaming – in broad daylight, in the middle of the park. Joggers and dog walkers all went about their business, ignoring my mum's cries as she begged for help. I can still hear the gurgling laughter of the woman whenever I shut my eyes and remember that dream.

Like before, it grew longer every night – and this time it did take months. Months and months of the same dream that built, night by night, to a crashing, hideous, gut-punching climax. And the next morning at break-fast, there was just two of us. Me and Dad.

I asked him, obviously. Well, I screamed at him. But no matter what I said, no matter what I asked, he just looked confused. Lost. Like he'd never even met Mum. Or maybe like someone had cut out every bit of his brain that knew anything about her. But it wasn't just that he couldn't remember, it was like the very idea of me having a mum was totally ridiculous. Like *I* needed to explain to *him* about the birds and the bees.

My gran moved in after that. And thank heaven she did, because just a few weeks later, I started having another dream. And by Christmas, it was just me and Gran. Just like that. In less than a year both Mum and Dad had gone. Gone forever, and gone *from* ever. Like they'd never existed. There's not one photo, not one diary or letter or email or text – not one thing to show they'd ever, ever existed.

Except me.

I ask Gran about them sometimes, but she won't talk. She just gets tearful, as if she's half remembering, but mainly forgetting. Then she looks worried. And I hate it when she looks worried. I still dream about them, and I can draw them. I can draw them exactly – down to the very last detail. In fact, I draw them all the time. And those hundreds of drawings are all I have left of them.

You never get used to it, losing your parents. Even adults say that. A dozen times a day you think about them – even when they've been gone for years. You think about telling them what you've done that day, or you think of a question you want to ask. You even expect to see them when you walk into a room. Expect to see them sitting there, smiling. But they never are. There's just an empty space where they should have been.

Now, you're probably thinking, 'Uh-oh, I wouldn't fancy being Gran much, bet she's next.' And I did too. For years I was a total mess – going to bed every night *expecting* a new dream – where the woman with the blood-red nails would come for Gran. Sometimes I tried to stay awake, but it never worked. I still had dreams, of course – creepy, scary, monstery dreams mainly – but the woman, she never came for Gran. And as primary school ticked on, things got a bit more normal. Christmases came and birthdays went, and my gran just, well, stuck around.

By the time I changed schools, life was actually pretty good. Gran's brilliant – she's like a normal parent, just older and more chill – about everything: homework, table manners, getting into trouble, everything. Gran's all about having fun, and being kind. She says life's too short to worry about anything else.

I even got used to the nightmares eventually. I'm not saying they're exactly fun. When stuff happens in my dreams it can bleed over into the real world – and that's pretty scary. If I get a cut or a bruise in a dream, I sometimes wake up like that. But it got to a point where I knew how to stay alive. When the monsters came – no matter how long I had to hide, or how fast I had to run – I always got away.

By the time I hit twelve, I'd almost started thinking I was safe. But then, right at the end of Year 7, I started having new dreams, about a girl.

And everything changed.

Each night would start the same, with the girl sitting on my window sill, the window open to the night sky. I'd never met her before. And she was like no girl I'd *ever* met before. Older than me, taller than me. And totally awesome and scary all at the same time.

They were flying dreams, all of them. She'd lead and I'd follow. And we'd go everywhere. And I mean *everywhere*. To flat-topped mountains covered in jungle, and volcanic lakes filled with flamingos. One time we flew all night and arrived to see the sun rise over the Himalayas. Sometimes she tried to speak, but it was like she was mute, or I was deaf, because no sound ever came out of her mouth. Each night she'd show me something new – a sea cave in a hidden cove, or an ancient tomb lost in the desert. Always something new, every night, the whole summer long.

The monsters were still there but, somehow, they weren't as frightening with her around. Her fighting was part of it. She could literally fight them off, and with impossible skills, like the hero in a martial arts movie. Leaping and spinning and kicking, sometimes faster than I could even see. For the first time in my life I felt part of a team, like I wasn't facing all those creatures alone. It even got to the point where I started looking forward to sleep.

But then the summer holidays ended and I went back to school. And on that first day back, there she was, the girl, in the lunch queue with the Year 9s. She looked at me, stared at me, and I couldn't stop staring back. Then she asked one of the other girls a question, and pointed at me.

And nothing's quite been the same ever since.

3

THE NEW GIRL

'She's way out of your league.'

For a split second I thought it was a voice in my head – but it wasn't. My best mate, Squid, said out loud what I should have been thinking.

'What do you mean?' I said defensively.

'That new girl. She's way out of your league. You know it.'

He was right of course. And then one of the Year 11 boys went up to her and started talking, and that sealed it. If James 'Call me Sully' O'Sullivan – all-round sports-action hero, future head boy and total git – was interested, then she really was way out of my league.

'Told you,' said Squid. 'The big fish are out.'

Sully said something and the girl smiled. So far, so

normal. When Sully speaks, all the girls smile. But then she turned her back on him. And no one's done that, like, probably ever.

She didn't see it, but the look on his face was pure gold. That may sound petty, but you don't know what it's been like. Sully's the sort of alpha kid who gets his kicks out of squashing the betas. And we were *way* below beta. We were right down with the omegas – or zetas – or whatever comes last in the whole secondary-school pecking-order hell.

It took me a while to realise she was back smiling again. And even longer to realise she was smiling across the hall at us. At *me*.

'Oh God, she's actually smiling at you,' said Squid. 'Do you know her?'

'Of course I don't know her.'

'Then why's she smiling at you?'

'I've no idea,' I lied, because even then I had the strangest feeling that she recognised me – from the dreams.

'Go up to her.'

I broke eye contact with the girl and turned to Squid. 'Are you insane? She's a Year Nine. And Sully's there.'

'So? She's smiling at you, not him. Just do it.'

'And say what?'

'Anything – it doesn't matter. It's called *first mover kudos* – making a first move is a massive sign of confidence. It puts you in the top two per cent for social status.'

Something you need to know about Squid is that he reads a lot. I mean a LOT. He even learned to play the flute from a book. Which is, like, totally old school. But his favourite thing is psychology books. I tell you, he's freakishly well informed for a kid. He can tell what someone's thinking just from the way they move their hands, or touch their face, or point their feet. He's like a flute-playing Sherlock Holmes trapped in the body of an undersized, twelve-year-old geek.

'She likes you,' he said, staring at the girl. 'That's so weird.'

'What's weird about it?' I said, shoving him with my elbow. But I knew he was right. This girl was a year older than us, and she was at least ten years cooler.

'Oh no. She's coming over,' said Squid, and a nanosecond later the girl picked up her lunch tray and started across the dining hall. 'Are you *sure* you don't know her?'

I could hear panic in Squid's voice. For all the psychology theory, when it comes to actual practical experience – he's at zero.

'Shoulders back,' he whispered. 'Keep eye contact.'

We both went silent as she came closer. And for the last few seconds we just sat there – like ice creams watching a seagull.

'D'you two always look like that?'

She had an American accent. That was a shock, but my brain didn't really have time to think about it.

'Look like what?' I heard myself garble.

'Like you've seen a zombie.'

Squid laughed, way too loud, and I kicked him under the table.

'I just …' I didn't know what to say, so I just said it straight out: 'Do I know you?'

'Funny, that.' She smiled. 'I was thinking the same thing.' She sat down without being asked (she was obviously in the top two per cent for social status). 'It's Finn, right?'

I nodded. And then remembered Squid.

'This is Squid.'

'Squid?'

'I'm Benji,' he corrected me. 'I mean Ben, but everyone calls me Squid because of this.' He pointed at the birthmark on his cheek that looks like a dead squid.

'Oh yeah, I see what you mean,' she said, almost in admiration.

17

And that could easily have been the end of the conversation. Because I really could not think of a single thing to say at that point. Well, I wanted to say, 'What's going on? How d'you know my name? Have you been having the same dreams as me?' But that's not exactly the sort of thing you can ask at school lunch to someone you've never met before. Not without looking weird. Everyone in the school, from Sully down, was looking at us, and believe me, at my school, you don't want to look weird.

But the girl didn't seem to care who was looking at us.

'What are you doing after school tomorrow?' she asked.

'What?'

'After school – tomorrow – can you make detention?'

'Well, yeah. But I don't have a detention.'

'You do now. Throw your lunch at me.'

'What?'

Of all the things I could have expected her to say, that wasn't one.

'I said, throw your lunch at me.'

'What?'

But she didn't ask again. With an eye-roll, she

scooped up a handful of her own lunch – and threw it in my face. Veggie korma.

Now, since getting to secondary school, I've got used to being bullied. And not just Sully, it's a rough school. But this? Korma, right in the face? It just didn't make sense.

Then she stood, and grabbed the table and literally flipped it over. That made even less sense.

Plates, food, cups, trays – everywhere. And the table hit the floor with a massive thump, like a falling drum. It echoed round the dining hall, followed by a wave of cheers. Anyone not watching before sure was watching now.

She acknowledged the cheers with a raised hand, then bent down, grabbed some food off the floor, and smeared it over her face. *Her own* face.

Now, given what I've written so far, you'd be forgiven for thinking this was just one of my dreams. But trust me, this was real.

I sat there, still in my chair, like a fool, my face and uniform covered in food.

'Finnegan Quick!' A shout roared across the lunch hall and I didn't need to look up to guess which teacher was shouting: Mr McCluskey.

'What have you done now, you *degenerate*?!'

McCluskey is one of the deputy heads, and he hates my guts, for some reason.

I scrambled to my feet – knocking over my chair.

'What *on earth* do you think you're doing?' McCluskey looked from me to the upturned table. There was food and drink everywhere. Squid had somehow managed to slip over in it and was nursing a twisted knee.

'Benji Bunn – I might have guessed you'd be involved too. Detention, the pair of you.'

'But it was *her*,' said Squid, pointing at the girl.

The girl made a goofy smile and gave a little wave.

'And who are you?' said McCluskey, seeing her for the first time.

'Hi, I'm Cass,' she said simply, sounding like someone off a US TV show.

'Well, *Cass*, detention for you too. And clear this mess up or I'll drag your parents in.'

'No, don't, sir,' I said quietly. 'She didn't do anything. It was all my fault. They had nothing to do with it.'

Squid would get in massive trouble with his mum for a detention. Whereas Gran always thinks I'm a hero.

McCluskey looked at me, obviously not certain. He does a funny little thing with his mouth when he's thinking, like he's chewing the inside of his cheek. I had a dream about it once: he was shouting at me in PE, on one of the football pitches, and then he stopped shouting and started chewing his cheek. And he kept chewing and chewing until there was an actual hole in it and I could see his teeth and everything – literally see his teeth through the side of his face. Proper freaky.

Then I saw *what* he was chewing: a giant black beetle that kept wriggling around in his mouth even when he crushed it between his teeth. It just wouldn't die, and eventually it crawled out of the side of his face, right up into his ear, and disappeared. Like it was burrowing all the way into his brain. Way beyond gross, I can tell you.

Every time I see him chewing his cheek, I remember that dream, and it turns my stomach.

McCluskey stood looking at me, chewing, thinking. Another couple of seconds and he might have changed his mind and let Squid and the girl get away with it. He's always up for sticking the blame on me.

But he didn't get those seconds. Because the girl, obviously determined to get a detention, calmly reached down and picked up what was left of Squid's cheese-burger. And with the smallest of smiles she lobbed it, underarm, right on to McCluskey's chest. Point-blank range. All over his shirt and tie.

I've never seen anyone go so red so fast. Even his neck went red, and then beyond red, into purple. His jaw muscles were working double speed — like that beetle was back. But he didn't say a word. He was so angry it was like he couldn't even speak.

'See you tomorrow,' said the girl. And she winked at me as she said it. Then walked away. The whole, entire school just watched in awed silence as she walked across the dining hall and out into the corridor.

'Did she just wink at you?' said Squid finally as we watched her disappear.

But I was totally lost for anything to say.

You can imagine how I felt going to bed that night. I couldn't wait to see her. To see if she'd now talk to me. I lay back and shut my eyes, eager for sleep for the first time in, like, ever. In my head, I practised conversations, over and over.

'Hi, Cass,' I said, smiling casually. 'Where to tonight?' In my mind I stood tall, with shoulders back and smiling eyes locked on to hers.

That's how I fell asleep, grinning from ear to ear. Imagining a hundred things.

But I woke shouting — screaming in terror. Because that night I had my first dream about Gran.

I call it the Goblin Dream.

4

THE GOBLIN DREAM

The Goblin Dream is a 'loop nightmare': a dream where the end is the same as the beginning, so you never know where it really starts, or truly ends. It's the worst kind of nightmare there is, because you're never sure that it even does end. And maybe the rest of my life from that point on has just been one never-ending nightmare.

I woke shouting – sitting up in bed like I'd been electrocuted. It was more of a bellow than a scream. The sort you'd use to scare away a wild animal. I was already looking around my room, and immediately knew something was different – *wrong* different.

When I wake like that normally, Gran's already shuffling across the landing to my bedroom. She seems to know I'm having a bad dream even before I cry out. And she always gives a little knock before coming in. A little rappity-tap-tap, so I know it's her. At that point we normally go down to the kitchen and she makes hot drinks.

But this night there was no shuffling, no rappity-tap. The whole house was quiet.

My first thought was to duck back under the duvet (it always is). But something about that silence made me realise I couldn't. I had to go and investigate.

There's always a light on at the top of the stairs. Gran bought a little red plug-light so you can see your way to the bathroom. But the landing is big and wide, and full of shadows. I never leave my bedroom, not normally. But tonight something drove me towards Gran's room.

We live in an old farm cottage, with wonky floors and creaking doors – but tonight the door to my gran's bedroom swung open in oily silence. Her wooden floor is covered in layers of rugs to keep out the cold, and I stepped on to them, edging into the black room.

My eyes are bad at night – Squid always jokes that I'm half blind when the sun goes down – and it took them ages to adjust to the moonlit gloom. But as my pupils grew bigger, and the shape on Gran's bed started to form, it was all I could do not to scream out for a second time.

Because there on Gran's sleeping chest, squatting like a little child, was a thick-bodied goblin. Its bald head and pointed ears shining in the moonlight. Its mouth was lowered towards Gran's face. Long finger-nails delicately stroked her cheeks. And with a sudden, heart-thudding realisation, I saw that it was *feeding* – sucking a pale green light from her mouth.

Then the goblin stopped. And turned its head towards me. As if it had known all along that I'd been standing there watching. It smiled long teeth, as if we were sharing a joke. And this time, I did scream.

I woke shouting – sitting up in bed like I'd been electrocuted. Like the nightmare had looped back to the beginning.

I sat there with my heart thumping, wondering if I'd go through the whole thing again, over and over, until it drove me mad. But then I heard Gran shuffling across the landing, and her rappity-tap-tap on my door.

'It's just a dream, Finnegan,' said Gran's voice. 'Come on, let's get you a nice hot drink.'

We went down to the kitchen and Gran made Horlicks. It's this weird, old-fashioned drink she makes that no one else has ever heard of. But over the years

I've come to quite like it. There's something about it that makes me think of biscuits.

'So what was after you this time? Werewolves? Zombies?' asked Gran, knowing I wouldn't answer.

I never answer, and she's OK with that. But she still asks anyway, to show she cares.

'It was just … you know, the same old same old.'

I could see disappointment in her eyes. After seven years of nightmares, of waking her most nights, I'd just stopped. Eight weeks ago, when the girl turned up on my window sill, I'd just stopped.

I obviously hadn't told Gran about the girl – that's not the sort of thing you talk to your grandmother about – but I guess she'd kind of started hoping the nightmares were over. I know I had.

And now she knew they weren't.

And so did I.

'I think maybe I'm just a bit stressed about going back to school.'

'Maybe you should quit,' she said with a big smile.

I'm never quite sure whether Gran's joking or not. She's got this weird sense of humour. I mean, she's seventy-odd but into practical jokes – not exactly normal old-person behaviour.

'I got a detention today.'

I hadn't told her before – but now seemed as good a time as any. And she wasn't much fazed by it. She never is.

'Who was it this time?' she asked, and looked pleased when I told her, 'McCluskey.'

'That weasel, he shouldn't be allowed anywhere near kids. He's a monster. What did you do?'

'Food fight,' I said, smiling. I knew she'd like that, and she did – laughing with a great big cackle.

'I hope you got McCluskey right in the face.'

'Not quite, and it wasn't his fault. He had to give me a detention; I totally deserved it.'

The last time McCluskey had put me down for a detention I *hadn't* deserved it. Gran had gone into school to give him an earful. And whatever he'd said to her clearly wasn't good enough, because in the school car park, on the way out, she'd stuffed tissues into the exhaust pipe of his sports car. A breakdown truck had to come, and everything. No one found out who'd done it, thankfully – but I didn't want to risk it happening again.

Gran had gone quiet; she looked serious.

'They will stop,' she said finally. 'You do believe that? Everyone grows out of night terrors. Not just most people … *Everyone.*'

Gran's a scientist. Well, a science teacher. Well, she used to be, when she was younger. And even though that's got nothing to do with nightmares, she's spent years reading research papers on anything and everything to do with sleep. Trying to find a solution to my 'little problem', as she still calls it. She's basically become a total expert.

'I do believe it, Gran. I promise.'

'Was it bad?' she asked, taking my hands in hers. 'It sounded bad.'

I nodded, not trusting my voice, but eventually said, 'It was worse than ever, Gran.'

For a moment I thought we were both going to cry. I saw tears in her eyes, but it may have been a reflection from the kitchen lights, because when she blinked, they were gone.

'Well,' she said, giving my hands a final squeeze. 'No point sitting down here hiding. Let's get you back to bed.'

I knew what was coming next; it's what she always says when it's time to stop drinking Horlicks and go back to bed.

'Remember, you've got to face your fears sometime, boy, or they'll bite you on the bum.'

'I wouldn't want that, Gran,' I said, getting up from

the table. And for a moment it felt like everything would be OK.

But then, at the bottom of the stairs, she stopped.

I could see her face, but it was blank, uncertain. She held up a hand and looked at it, like she'd never seen one before. I looked at it too, and saw how old it was.

Then she looked at me. But it was like she couldn't see me, or was looking through me, like I wasn't there. She blinked and her eyes were suddenly different. And that's when I knew we were doomed. Because the eyes that looked across at me – well, there's no other way of saying it – *those eyes weren't hers.*

And in that moment, as the eyes smiled at me, I knew with total certainty that they'd come for Gran. The Goblin Dream would grow, would take my gran, night by night, until there was nothing left. It might take weeks or months, but sooner or later, there'd be nothing left. Nothing left of the kindest, warmest, funniest person I'd ever known. All the jokes and stories and funny little sayings and clever ideas – all gone.

And I'd be just me, alone, in an empty house.

She shook her head, blinking violently. And just like that, her eyes were back to normal. And so was Gran.

'Come on, the sun will be up before you know it.'

I went back to bed with one thought: they were coming for Gran and the only way to survive this – the only way to keep her safe – was to stay awake.

I can never sleep again, I decided.

Ever.

5

THE NEXT DAY

I went back to bed and I didn't sleep. Dawn was already coming up, and with my heart thumping and my head spinning there was no way I could have slept, even if I'd wanted to.

I got up early and was out the door before Gran was even awake. She likes to sleep in and I just couldn't face her that morning. I wasn't sure I could face anything.

The school day dragged on like usual. The normal pick'n'mix of teachers: some annoyingly grumpy, some annoyingly jolly. I'm never sure which is worse: teachers who like to hear their own shouting, or teachers who pretend they're your bestie.

But I couldn't really focus on any of it – even Squid at breaktime jabbering on about his latest research (some rubbish about 'how to make a dynamite first impression'). It all just seemed to slide off my brain.

Instead, I spent the day thinking about Gran (one minute) and Cass (the next). Until suddenly it was the end of the school day, time for detention. And all I could think about was Cass.

Now, detention is always in the Hardy Block, the science block at the back of the school and across from the staffroom. I'm not sure why, but I guess it's so the teacher who supervises can bunk off and put their feet up. That's what always happens, and it means detentions can be risky. Think of it like a dodgy prison movie. You can find yourself stuck alone in there with *anyone*, and more often than not it's some angry Year 11 who wants to see if they can lift you up by the head.

But today, I guess being only the second day of term, it was just the three of us. Me, Squid and Cass.

McCluskey gave his usual lecture, then set us lines – the most pointless punishment in the universe. The sort of thing they did in schools a hundred years ago. And then he left, probably to put his feet up in the staffroom.

I looked across at Cass. Now was the moment I'd been thinking about all day. I'd finally learn what this was all about. But she just sat there, writing out the first line.

'*Fighting during lunch is disgusting and thoughtless behaviour, and shows disrespect for other members of the school community,*' she wrote. And then looked across at me and Squid.

'Come on. The clock's ticking.' Her American accent seemed to have softened. Or maybe I was just getting used to it.

Squid looked at me with raised eyebrows, and, a bit annoyed, I started writing too. Was this it? Were we just gonna sit here in detention and do lines for the whole hour?

'OK, that's enough. You just need one line. Squid can do the rest.'

'What?' said Squid. He hadn't even finished his first line.

'You, Squid, are going to copy our handwriting. So get a hurry on.'

'But I can't do all of it,' he complained.

'Do as much as you can,' said Cass, and jumping up, crossed to the outside door to peer through the glass.

'OK, Finnegan Quick,' she said, satisfied that McCluskey had gone. 'There's somewhere else you need to see.'

Somewhere else. I felt my brain fizz.

'It *is* you,' I said, and she nodded.

33

'Of course it is.'

Now, Squid isn't normally one to speak up, he's pretty shy, but even he couldn't keep quiet after hearing that.

'What do you mean, "It *is* you"?'

Cass looked at Squid, and then at me. 'Do you want to tell him?'

'We've met before,' I said.

'I knew it!' said Squid accusingly. 'I totally knew it. There's no way she'd have talked to you if she hadn't met you before.'

'We haven't met before,' countered Cass. 'Not in real life. We've just met ... in our dreams.'

Squid raised his eyebrows. 'You mean you *like* each other?'

'No!' I interrupted. 'She means in an actual dream. Well, loads of actual dreams. Over the summer.'

I've told Squid a fair bit about my dreams. Not everything, obviously – not the bit about them sometimes coming true. But he knows I dream a lot. I tell him all the gory stuff and he loves it. The freakier the better.

'This is gonna sound weird,' I explained, 'but over the summer I started having dreams about a girl I'd never met before.' I nodded towards Cass. 'And then she showed up yesterday.' I paused to let it sink in. 'I know it sounds crazy, but it's true.'

34

'OK, we don't have time for this. You, Squid, get on with the lines – Finnegan, come with me.'

'Why?' I asked, suddenly nervous. A lot of my dreams start off like this. All excitement. But they quickly turn dark.

'I need to show you something.'

'Show me what?'

'Something. Everything. Show you what's happened. Why you're having these dreams.'

I must have pulled a face, or maybe I just looked blank, because she seemed annoyed.

'I think I know where they are,' she said softly. 'Your parents. I can show you what happened to your parents.'

After that I really did look blank.

'If you want answers, I can show you. Now. But it's only safe if we do it in the chemistry lab. We need the right equipment.'

'But ...' Squid started, but he didn't finish.

Cass had reached the corridor and she turned back to him. 'Just shut up and do the lines, Squid.' Then she looked at me. 'Are you coming?'

I sat there. It felt like my brain cells were dissolving into soup. She disappeared into the gloomy corridor and I looked at Squid.

'*No way*,' he mouthed, shaking his head. Then he whispered, 'Finn, just don't. Don't trust her.'

But the girl's words kept throbbing through my head. Like I was hearing them over and over: *I can show you what happened to your parents.*

I thought about Biscuit. Maybe I'd see what happened to him too.

And then I thought of Gran, and suddenly I was standing.

'Are you insane?' said Squid. 'The chemistry lab? She probably wants to blow the school up or something.'

'Don't be stupid. Why would she do that?'

'I don't know. Maybe she's from some secret religious cult.'

'Seriously? You read way too much.'

'I'm just saying.' Squid pulled a face. 'And what do I say if McCluskey comes back?'

But I wasn't listening.

'I've got to,' I said, without even looking at hm. And then followed Cass into the gloomy corridor.

6

THE CHEM LAB

She was waiting, obviously annoyed, at the end of the corridor outside the chem lab. So I ran, and together we went inside.

The first surprise was that Cass had somehow already set things up. At the back of the classroom, half hidden behind the teacher's desk, was a pile of cushions spread out on the floor.

I don't know what I thought. And I must have just stood there, frozen, because she gave me a shove.

'Fill those buckets with warm water,' she said, pointing at two buckets that I hadn't even noticed. 'Use this thermometer and get them to forty degrees. *Exactly* forty, understand?'

I didn't argue. There's a whole row of sinks in the

chem lab, and I started filling both buckets. But all the time I couldn't take my eyes off her. She was busy on her phone, but not for long. Then she disappeared into the walk-in cupboard at the back of the lab. It's where they store all the chemicals, and it's always locked. But she just walked right in, like she had a key.

She came out carrying a plastic bottle and a glass flask. The bottle had a bunch of red warning symbols on it.

'Buckets over here,' she said, nodding towards the cushions on the floor. 'One on each side.'

And maybe it was the way she said it – like she was ordering a dog about – or maybe it was something else, but I decided I'd had enough of all the *Scooby-Doo* mystery stuff.

'Are you going to tell me what's going on?' I said, putting the buckets back down in the sink and turning to face her.

'Look, if you can just trust me – I can show you. But we don't have time to go through it all first.'

'No, I need to know what this is all about.'

She looked at the clock, and her face softened.

'OK, you can have three questions – but then we've got to go.'

'OK.' It felt good to be standing up to somebody for once. '*Who are you?*'

'I'm Cass, I already told you. Is that really your first question?'

'Oh, come on. You know what I mean. Why have you been in my dreams all summer?'

'Is *that* your first question?'

'Yes … please.' There was something about this girl that made you want to say please.

'I was just training you up a bit. You know, helping you to stop running away at the first sign of danger.'

'I do not run away at the first sign of danger.'

'Well, you kind of do. I mean, you did – you're better now. You're ready.'

I thought about all the dreams we'd had together. All the places we'd been.

'So if that was all just training …' I tried to hide the disappointment from my voice. 'What's next?'

'Is that question two?' she asked, and I shook my head.

With only three questions, I had to think clearly. Eventually I came up with, 'Question two is: why are you doing all this?'

'That's easy. It's my job – well, it's my dad's job – to investigate, and I'm helping him out.'

'You expect me to believe you're from some sort of dream police?'

'I don't expect you to believe anything. And we're obviously not police – that would be ridiculous. We're more like … investigators. We investigate unusual paranormal activity.'

'Isn't all paranormal activity unusual? It's kind of in the definition of paranormal.'

'Is that your third question?'

'No. You still haven't answered question two. Why are you doing this?'

'OK, let's just say we investigate *interesting* paranormal events – not just the run-of-the-mill ghost stuff, or all those million UFOs. My dad's only interested in the good stuff. You know, bleeding statues, dead people coming back to life, disappearing villages, that sort of thing.'

'Disappearing villages?' I wasn't sure whether she was laughing at me.

'Yeah, sure, why not. Happens all the time. You've heard of Brigadoon, right? The village that reappears for one day every hundred years.'

'I thought that was just a movie,' I said softly.

'It was – but based on a real legend. It happens a lot. Russia alone has lost about twenty.'

'So now you're investigating me.'

'Yeah, *you* are off-the-charts unusual.' Cass rubbed her eye impatiently.

'What do you mean?' I asked, not sure I wanted to hear the answer.

'You know your mum and dad didn't just disappear, don't you? They disappeared so hard and so *far*, they never even existed. That's pretty spectacular.'

I felt a sudden rush of blood into my neck. This was a lot to take in. For a second I couldn't speak.

'Are we done? Or do you have a final question?'

I knew exactly what my final question was.

'Why now?'

'What do you mean?'

'My mum and dad disappeared seven years ago. So why now?'

Cass shrugged. 'I guess you finally got to the top of Dad's to-do list. Congrats.'

I wanted to believe her, but I couldn't help noticing that she didn't look me in the eyes when she said it.

'Look, we're out of time. If you can just trust me, I can show you. Otherwise, this is all a complete waste of time. Are you in?'

She picked up a box of matches.

'Oh hell. Squid was right. You *are* going to blow the school up.'

'Stop being so hysterical. This is just to make double sure we wake up.' She tipped out the matchbox into the glass flask. Not the matches, just the heads, like she'd cut them off with a knife. They formed a little red mound at the bottom of the glass flask. Then she opened the bottle.

'Ammonia,' she said, pouring it into the flask. Then she set the flask on to a tripod above a burner. And lit it.

'What?' she said, clearly amused by the look on my face. 'It's a stink alarm.'

'You mean a stink bomb?'

'No, *alarm*. A stink bomb is an actual bomb. Invented by Leonardo da Vinci five hundred years ago to defeat ships attacking Venice. The stink *alarm* ... I invented five seconds ago.' She turned down the burner. 'This will get full-on rank in about twenty minutes. At about the same time the water in those buckets will get cold. Cold enough to make you want to go to the restroom. So if you smell rotten eggs or you need to pee – that's your reminder to wake up, that it's just a dream. Got it?'

'What's wrong with a phone alarm?'

'I've set that too, but sounds don't always work, not if the dream's, you know, *intense*.'

She looked at the flask. Little bubbles were already starting to form on the glass.

'Come on, we're losing time, get the buckets over here.'

Now I had a fourth question: what could be so *intense* we wouldn't hear an alarm? But for some reason I didn't ask. I just carried over the buckets, and put them down either side of the cushions.

'Lie down,' said Cass. And I did that too.

'Put your hand in the bucket. Shut your eyes and listen to the white noise.'

A loud humming-hiss came out of her phone and she placed it above my head. I shut my eyes.

Then I heard her lowering herself on to the cushions next to me, and felt her shoulder press against mine. My eyes pinged open, and I turned to see her face only inches from mine.

'Are you gonna tell me where we're going?' I asked, not really sure I was ready to hear the answer.

'We're going to sleep together,' she said simply, then laughed. A childish laugh that made her look younger. 'Dream yourself right here, OK?' Her face went suddenly serious. 'Now shut your eyes and go to sleep.'

'Is this dangerous?' I asked, and immediately wished I hadn't.

'Hell, yeah.'

She laughed again, but only for a moment. 'Look, I know you're scared, but think of it as an adventure. It's just a dream, it'll be fun.'

43

I wasn't having that. 'You don't understand,' I said. 'My dreams – they're not like normal dreams.'

'I know. I've been there, remember?'

'*No*,' I said, more fiercely than I meant to. 'Things that happen in my dreams … sometimes they don't stay in my head.'

I'd never said that before. Not to anyone.

I expected a load of questions, but she just said, 'I know. Trust me, I get it.'

'What do you mean, *you get it*? You *can't* get it. No one *gets it*. If someone dies in one of my dreams, they stay dead.'

'No, trust me, I get it,' she repeated, and reached out to touch my arm. I suddenly realised I'd been holding my breath.

'How? How are you not totally weirded out by that?'

'For a very simple reason.' She smiled, pushing me back down on to the cushions. 'The same thing used to happen to my mum. Before she died.'

I shut up then.

'Just dream about being here in the lab, OK?' said Cass. 'And remember, you can talk and hear in dreams. You just have to believe it.'

And that was it. Before I could even think about that, she'd shut her eyes and crossed her arms over her chest like a vampire in a coffin. For all I know, she was asleep two seconds later.

My head was spinning. I was on the floor with a Year 9 girl pressed up against me, shoulder to shoulder. My hand was in a bucket of water and a Bunsen burner was firing away just above my head. Nothing about this was normal.

But then, nothing about my life's ever been normal.

I thought of Mum and Dad. Then I thought of Gran, wondered how many weeks or months she had left. Because I knew, deep down, that I didn't have a choice. Not really. This girl, psycho or not, was my only hope. And besides, I remember thinking, it can't be worse than the Goblin Dream.

What an idiot.

The loud hiss thrumming out of her phone seemed to jostle my brain into submission. I was tired. I'm always tired. And as I lay there, thinking about her shoulder pressing into mine, my mind slipped away.

Into sleep.

7

THE CHEM LAB DREAM

My eyes flicked open and I sat up. Cass was already standing and she pulled me to my feet, nodding towards the clock on the far wall. For a moment I didn't understand, and then I did. The second hand was running backwards, anticlockwise. We were asleep – and this was just a dream.

I looked down and saw our bodies – eyes shut, peacefully sleeping. The burner was firing heat into the glass flask and the bubbles in the ammonia were getting bigger.

Her mouth moved but no sound came out. She rolled her eyes and pointed angrily at it with both hands. '*Come on,*' she seemed to be mouthing, and I immediately remembered: *You can talk and hear in dreams. You just have to believe it.*

Did I believe it? I wasn't sure.

She kept trying to talk, but her mouth was moving so fast I couldn't even begin to lip-read. I just about made out the word 'idiot' before she slapped me in the face. Hard. Like a proper punch: hard. Then she raised her arm to do it again.

'Stop!' I shouted, and she smiled, dropping her arm.

'See, you just needed to believe it,' she said, pulling me towards the door. 'Come on, we don't have much time.'

My dreams with Cass up to that point had always been flying dreams. And I expected us to fly now. But we ran. Ran across the empty playground to the school gate, through the car park and on to the road into town.

The school is in open countryside on a hill overlooking the town. It's new, even though the town itself is old. Dewkesbury sits on the River Avon in a narrow valley and it's been there since ancient times, forgotten by just about everybody. It's bigger than it was in the Dark Ages, but not by much – the valley's so tight there's nowhere really to build.

Cass ran ahead and I struggled to keep up. She just seemed to skim across the ground, hardly touching the pavement. Other than that, it was easy to forget this was just a dream. At four o'clock on a school day, everything was boring normal. The sky was blue; the sun was yellow. Parents drove kids home from school and old people walked their dogs. Nothing suggested this was a dream.

'Head for the church,' said Cass as we reached the edge of town.

The church is practically on the river and we reached it quickly, slowing to a walk at the gates. The crunch of the gravel path sounded loud.

'Not that way,' she said, stepping off the path on to a grass-covered grave.

I hate walking over graves. I don't know why, but I do. But with Cass threading her way between gravestones, I had no choice but to follow.

We crossed round the back of the church, on to the shady side next to the river, and I felt a shiver as the afternoon sun disappeared behind the big church spire. The graveyard goes on a long way; there must be hundreds buried there.

At the far end is a giant wall with an old wooden door set inside it, and beyond that, a big old manor house where some lord used to live. It's been empty for, like, a billion years, but everyone's got a story about it. Mainly about a woman they've seen – a ghost – looking out of the upstairs windows.

'We're not going in there?' I said, pointing.

'Why? What's wrong with there?'

'That's Freak House.'

She laughed. 'Why do you call it that?'

'You know, little things. Like there are bars on some of the upstairs windows.'

'Well, don't worry, we're going somewhere much freakier.'

My heart twisted when I saw where. Because on the far side of the cemetery, right next to the river, is a little stone building with big pillars and iron gates. All the local kids call it 'The Crypt', probably because, well, that's what it is: an old mausoleum full of dead people.

Cass stepped between the two stone columns and pulled on the iron gates. In real life they're always chained and padlocked – but in the dream they swung open with a gentle creak.

'OK, just stop. I'm not going one more step until you tell me what we're doing.'

She turned, clearly irritated, but managed to take in a breath before speaking. 'Your mum and dad aren't dead, they're trapped. And I think they're trapped in here. Is that enough for you?'

'No. I've got questions.'

'What questions?'

'Well. Firstly. How do you know?'

'It's complicated.'

A sudden wind blew through the churchyard, bending trees and kicking up leaves, strong enough to move the gates. They swung shut with an angry screech. Like a warning. It really didn't help.

'Look, I can explain it all later, but right now –' she looked at her watch – 'we've got about fifteen minutes before everything kicks off back at the lab.'

She stared at me, but I refused to look away.

'I've got more questions,' I said.

'I don't care,' she replied, turning back to the crypt. She paused for a moment, and took a final breath.

'Are you good?' she asked, without looking back.

I shook my head, but she didn't see, and without another word, she pulled back the gates and stepped inside.

Now, you probably think I'd have to be a total numbnut to go in there. After everything I've seen? After everything that's happened to me? Maybe I was just stupid back then. Maybe I still am. But the thought that I might see my parents, might see what happened to them, was too much. And for all her angry-teen vibe, there was something about Cass that told me I could trust her.

I stepped inside and was immediately hit by the smell of meat. It filled the back of my throat and I covered my mouth with an arm. It wasn't disgusting, exactly, not rotting meat, but fresh. Like the smell of a butcher's. But for some reason that was worse.

'Remember. This is a dream,' said Cass, and she suddenly had a mask around her neck. An old Covid mask that she pulled up over her face. 'Just dream what you need,' she said, pulling a second mask from her pocket and giving it to me.

I must have looked surprised because she laughed.

'It's a dream, idiot. You want it enough? You get it.' This time she pulled out a torch and lit up the far wall. There was an open doorway with stairs that led down.

The whole place was cold and damp and miserable. Why people want to be buried in places like that I've never understood. The stone steps were slick with green – moss or algae or whatever – so we trod carefully. Believe it or not, you can fall over in a dream, and when I do, I wake with bruises. So we went steady, lower and lower, until the stairway finally opened into a large underground space.

It was even colder now and, if anything, the air smelt worse, stronger. Like we were closer to the meat.

Cass's torch darted about, revealing great stone arches and a room that seemed to go on forever.

This isn't a room, it's a chamber, I remember thinking. If I'd dared to shout out, there'd have been an almighty echo. But I didn't dare.

Finally the torch came to rest on a massive stone object at the far end of the chamber. It was a stone coffin, a sarcophagus.

'Look at the walls.' Cass squeezed my shoulder and lifted the torch to show the far wall. It was filled with square alcoves, large cubbyholes, each big enough to hold a coffin. Cass held a finger to her lips and I didn't need to be told twice. Then she shone her light back on to the giant sarcophagus in the centre. And pushing her torch into my hand, she held up a shiny, black crowbar.

Her eyes smiled in delight.

'You've got to be kidding!' I whispered harshly, terrified by the loudness of my voice as it echoed back at me.

'This is what we came for, idiot.' She jammed the bent end of the crowbar into a small gap beneath the stone lid. 'If I'm right, your parents are in here.'

I wanted to say something, but I couldn't. My brain went into free fall as she jammed the crowbar into the gap. She levered it from side to side, forcing the metal between the lid and base.

Was I really about to see my mum and dad? Still alive, trapped inside this stone coffin for all these years? Were they sleeping? Would they look the same? Would they *be* the same?

The grinding of metal on stone told me I wouldn't have to wait long.

'Get the torch on this,' said Cass, and I immediately moved the light. She'd managed to inch the crowbar under the stone lid and was working it up and down, the lid inching open as she forced it deeper.

'Get another crowbar in there.'

'I don't have a crowbar,' I said stupidly, and she rolled her eyes theatrically.

'Then dream one up, moron.' Her voice was showing strain; the lid was heavy.

'How?'

But she never answered. Because at that exact moment, the torch began to flicker.

Cass looked at it in horror. 'Are you doing that?' she said, and I shook my head. And then, so quietly we almost didn't notice it, a solitary coffin began to move out of its vault in the far wall. We watched, frozen, as it slid gently towards us.

Then a second coffin began to move. And a third. They all slid smoothly, like they were gliding on runners.

And then the first coffin began to tip forwards, and with a sudden lurch it crashed to the floor. Wood splintered and the room echoed as we watched, dumb with horror. One by one, the coffins tilted and smashed – and still we just stood there, frozen.

Then a hand emerged from the shattered wood of the first coffin, then an arm. Ripping itself free of the splintered wood.

Cass didn't need me to tell her, but I shouted it anyway.

'*Run!*'

She was ahead of me all the way up the stairs. But she slipped near the top, and the sole of her boot smashed into my face. She couldn't have kicked me better if she'd tried. And I fell, slipping on the slime-covered steps. I can't have slid far, but I smacked the front of my head and it took me a moment to recover. And when I did, a hand was grabbing at my leg – squeezing tight around the bone of my ankle.

My left arm felt suddenly cold and I remember thinking, *It's sucking the life out of me.* But I never got to say a word, because the stink of sulphur was filling my nose and mouth and lungs.

The power of that hand as it pulled me downwards was terrifying. It was beyond human. But I screamed and kicked. Got free. And by some miracle was scrambling back up on hands and feet – crashing into Cass at the top.

'They're coming!' I shouted, but she wouldn't move. She just stood there, blocking my way. 'Just go!' I screamed, but she didn't move.

And then I saw why. The iron gates that led back into the graveyard were shut. And beyond them, silhouetted against the daylight, stood a figure. White, bloodless hands held them tight. Even without the red nails, I would have recognised them. The same hands that had snatched away my dog, Biscuit. The same woman who'd always been lurking in my nightmares. Those hands *squeezed* the bars together. Bending the metal until the iron twisted on to itself. Sealed tight forever.

Then the figure stepped backwards, and late afternoon sun shone across its face. After all these years I saw her face for the first time. And immediately wished I hadn't. It was bloody from a thousand tiny cuts, and blind from thick bandages wrapped around her eyes. Deep pockets of blood soaked through where her eyes should have been.

Cass screamed.

She'd not shown even a hint of fear before. And the sight of her screaming was possibly the most terrifying thing of all.

Then the torch flickered, and went out. In the dark I couldn't run and I couldn't hide. The stink of sulphur was unbearable – it burned into my lungs, so bad I couldn't breathe. Not even when hands started grabbing my clothes. They were dragging me backwards, down into the crypt. But I couldn't scream.

Not until I woke up.

I woke screaming, and with Squid shouting in my face.

He was shaking me, making it impossible to breathe. But I never got the chance to tell him, because Cass was screaming too.

Something was dragging her across the floor. An invisible *something* that had her by the feet. It was like I'd woken from one dream, right into another. Or maybe I was still half asleep.

I shoved Squid away and he fell back, his face stupid with shock. I tried to get to my feet, but I was slow. My arms, legs, everything was slow, like my brain was still only half awake.

And if Cass's head hadn't smacked on to the door frame I don't know what would have happened. But the sickening thud of her skull on the wooden frame seemed to jolt my own brain fully awake, and suddenly everything lurched into clarity.

I scrambled over to her, but she didn't stop screaming, even when I'd helped her get to her feet. She just screamed at me like I was a monster.

Then punched me in the face.

8

AFTERWARDS

Afterwards was a bit of a crap-show to be honest.
Maybe because of the screaming, or the stink bomb (sorry, Cass: stink *alarm*), or maybe he was just coming back anyway – but, basically, McCluskey showed up. Right then and right there. God knows what he thought we were up to. The really weird thing though was that he never asked.

I won't put you through another McCluskey tongue-lashing, but let's just say we earned ourselves a lot of cheek-chewing, another week of detentions, a letter to 'your parents or carers' and thirty minutes of cleaning up 'this *diabolical* mess'.

Except then he saw the cut on Cass's head, and had to take her to the school office to get it looked at. It was bleeding loads, and I guess he panicked, worried he'd get in trouble for leaving us unsupervised.

That left me with Squid's raised eyebrows.

'So, are you gonna tell me what just happened?'

'What do you mean?'

'Oh come on, I know what I just saw. This place looks like a bomb hit it. And it smells like … I don't know what it smells like.'

I could probably have just bluffed it out, and gone back to mopping the floor – but I didn't. It had felt good talking to Cass, telling her the truth. And looking now at Squid, I decided to tell him. What is it they say – the truth will set you free? It was time to tell my secret.

'OK, I've wanted to tell you for ages …'

He stood there, fake-smiling, expectant, silent.

'I don't dream like normal people,' I said. 'I can control what happens. Well, I can control what *I do* … in the dream. And so can Cass.'

'What, like lucid dreaming? Loads of people can do that. I even did it once. *This …*' He pointed at the smears of Cass's blood on the floor. 'This is *not* lucid dreaming.'

'No, it's a bit more than that. Sometimes my dreams, kind of, cross over – into real life. They change things.'

Squid looked at me, then at the mess on the floor. 'What?'

'Look, I know it sounds mad, but we were dreaming together. And I must have still been half asleep when that happened to Cass.'

I looked at the mess of cushions and overturned stools strewn across the floor, and then at the blood on the door frame where Cass had smashed her head.

'I still don't get what happened to Cass?'

I hesitated, struggling to think how to explain it. 'We were in a dream together. And some … *things* were dragging her away and so … well, it must have crossed over, into real life. You saw, right?'

Squid looked at me, then back down at the floor.

'I don't know what I saw,' he said.

'If you could just see what it's like being in one of my dreams, you'd understand. That's what Cass has been doing all summer.'

'How does that even work?' His look of horror and disbelief hadn't shifted an inch.

'I dunno, she just dreams herself in my bedroom, I guess.'

Now that would normally have got a snigger. But Squid just stood there, with a face full of revulsion.

McCluskey came back then, and I never got a chance to say anything else. Squid's mum had been phoned to come and collect him. I expect he got the rollicking of a lifetime. They probably tried to phone Gran too, but she's always out on Tuesdays. So I just cycled home on my own.

I had no idea what Squid thought. I tried to message him, to say sorry. But he didn't even open it.

And then, just after I'd gone up to bed, a reply came through.

It said: ?????

Which just about summed everything up.

I turned off my phone, and buried my head in a pillow.

9

THAT NIGHT

I was determined not to sleep. Totally.

If I didn't sleep, I wouldn't dream. And if I didn't dream, I couldn't dream about the crypt, or the woman with no eyes. And perhaps even more urgently, I couldn't dream about the goblin. And Gran.

But my track record on staying up all night? Well, let's just say it's a bit patchy.

It always happens the same way. I start off full of plans. I listen to podcasts, read a book, sometimes I draw. That all takes me to about midnight – and then I really struggle. That's when I usually think about a little power nap – just to give me a boost.

That night I set my phone alarm for fifteen minutes, just to be on the safe side. Nothing bad can happen in a quarter of an hour – is the theory. I checked the volume was up to max and shut my eyes. Determined to have the shortest nap possible.

I must have fallen asleep immediately, because when my eyes flicked open, I thought I was still awake. But the window was open, with Cass sitting on the ledge.

'No. Go away,' I said.

'Not until you meet someone.'

She looked older than she did in real life, I suddenly noticed.

'Do you mean my parents? Or maybe that woman without eyeballs?'

She leaned backwards, and for a second I thought she was going to apologise. I was still learning that Cass doesn't do apologies.

'We had some turbulence, that's all. Deal with it. We just need to regroup, learn and try again.'

That's when I noticed the rope, wrapped over her arm. 'Are you ready for a surprise?' she said, uncoiling it, then shouted out the window. 'Ready?'

She pulled with both arms but not much effort, and with a final yank a small figure tumbled into my room.

'Squid?! What are you doing here?'

Squid was just a collapsed bundle on the floor. He untangled himself from a massive brown dressing gown and sat himself up. If anything, he looked smaller than he did in real life. And for some reason he had his left hand up in the air – like he needed the toilet in class.

'Is that really you?' said Squid, getting to his knees. He still had one arm in the air – but with the other he reached out to touch my knee.

'This is so cool. How is this even happening? I can actually feel you.' He looked up at me with an enormous smile. 'You even feel like you.'

He looked at me and the smile slowly slid off his face. 'OK, I get it. We need to focus. What's next?'

'Go home, Squid. That's what's next.' I looked at Cass; she was smiling, and that just made me even more annoyed. 'You had no right dragging him into this.'

'I haven't dragged him anywhere. He was here before I was.'

'Then how did he get here?' I didn't even try to hide my anger.

'I took a bus.'

'You took the bus?' Cass even laughed as she said it.

'OK, that's brilliant work, buddy, but you need to go home.'

'Why has he got one arm in the air?' asked Cass.

'Good question.' I turned to Squid. 'Why have you got your arm in the air?'

'It's a lucid dreaming technique I found—'

'Not one I've ever seen,' interrupted Cass.

'Squid, you don't need to keep it up the whole time,' I said.

Squid put his arm down. 'The book said it would fall down after I fell asleep. It's supposed to wake me up just enough that I remember to take control of the dream. That's how I got here.'

'OK, do you know how to get the bus back?'

'This is so awesome,' said Squid, still prodding my arm. Then he stopped, and looked up at me. 'I still don't get it though.'

'Which bit?'

'Well, I understand the lucid dreaming stuff. With the right techniques your brain can stay conscious enough to dream whatever you want. According to the book, anyone can do that – with the right techniques.'

'So which bit don't you get?' repeated Cass, showing some impatience.

'The bit about us all being here, in the same dream. How does that work?'

Cass was clearly irritated. 'It's simple. If you and somebody else dream yourself in the same place, at the same time, you actually meet them there.'

'But why? How?'

'That's just how it works.'

'Then why doesn't this happen all the time?'

'It probably does. But people just don't realise it. Having awesome dreams is easy – the hard bit is remembering them.'

'Is that what's special about you and Finn? You can remember your dreams?'

But she never answered. Because at that precise moment a door banged somewhere in the house. Squid flinched.

'What was that?' he asked pointlessly.

Then another bang – maybe the same door, opening and slamming. And then again. And again.

'I think you got a ghost,' said Cass, smiling at the look of horror on Squid's face.

'No, not a ghost,' I said quietly. 'A goblin.'

'A goblin? That's so cool. Are all your dreams like this?' Squid got to his feet and started towards the door. 'Come on,' he said. 'What are we waiting for? This is just a dream – it's totally safe. We can do anything we want. Let's be heroes.'

'I wouldn't do that, mate. We just need to leave it alone.' Something about the way I said it made Squid pause.

I didn't quite know what to say next, and in the end Cass said it for me.

'Being a hero in one of his dreams isn't as easy as you might think.'

'Why?'

'Let's just say there's a lot of nasties around. And they do more than give you a bad dream.' She pointed at the gash on the side of her head, where she'd hit the chemistry lab door frame.

'Squid, you know I said earlier that things in my dreams sometimes cross over into real life? Well, it means that if you break a leg in one of my dreams you could wake up with a broken leg. Lose an eye and you might actually lose an eye.'

Squid's face went blank. Like his brain had lost its Wi-Fi connection.

'And if that goblin eats you,' finished Cass, 'there's a decent probability that you'll stay eaten.'

Squid's brain seemed to be slowly getting back online; he looked at me, appalled.

'But that's not possible.' Squid visibly flinched back from the door. He looked at me like I was a monster. And in that moment, I felt our friendship start to dissolve. Like I always knew it would if anyone ever discovered the truth about me.

'Rare,' said Cass, 'but not impossible.'

I nodded. 'Sorry, mate. You should probably go.'

He looked at me, and for a second I thought I saw more than fear. I thought I saw *disgust*.

But then a shaky grin broke back out. The famous, slightly lopsided Squid grin. The one that always makes him look like a toddler filling a nappy.

'I'm cool,' he said eventually, nodding his head and looking anything but.

Cass was obviously getting impatient. 'Come on then, chickies, let's show some backbone. Squid, if you're nervous, stay at the back.' She pushed past Squid and into the doorway.

'I'm not going either,' I blurted out, forcing her to look back. 'You don't understand. There's something trying to get Gran. And if I see it happen … it happens.' Gran's bedroom door banged again, and I felt myself twitch.

'Look, we've got this,' said Cass.

'You said that this afternoon. And look what happened,' I said, staring at the wound across the side of her head.

'You just don't get it, do you? You can't hide under the duvet all your life.'

'Maybe I can,' I said, wishing more than anything that I was right. 'Maybe I *have to*. You don't understand. Gran is all I've got left. If they take her – I've got nothing.'

She turned away from us and, without looking back,

said, 'You asked me earlier why I've been in your dreams all summer. What the training has all been about.'

I nodded. I wasn't so sure I wanted to hear this.

'Well, the only way you're going to find your mum and dad … is if you can learn to stop hiding all the time.' She turned to Squid and said, 'The training's taking longer than we thought,' before disappearing on to the landing.

'Ouchie!' said Squid. 'You just been *burned*, buddy.'

He was right, but I should have just ignored it. I should have stayed. But like an idiot, I followed Cass out of my bedroom door.

Now, this didn't feel liking a turning point at the time. After all, I was just going out of my bedroom door. Like I'd done, what, ten thousand times before? But it was.

In my head, I knew this was a really bad idea. But there was something about Cass's confidence – and Squid's too, in his own way. It made me feel, not brave exactly, but something on the way to brave: hopeful.

With the benefit of hindsight, I should have ducked under the duvet and stayed there for, maybe, ever. But instead I listened to that stupid little voice of hope and followed Cass out of my bedroom door.

She was already at the far end of the big landing. Even with only the red plug-light I could see all I needed to. The door to Gran's bedroom was banging away with a steady beat. Each time it would open slowly, then slam shut fast. And I knew exactly what was happening. The goblin was goading us, toying with us, *luring* us towards my gran's room.

We caught up with Cass and she gave me a silent look, then grabbed the door before it could shut. I don't think she was expecting the force of it, because she suddenly needed two hands and a foot to keep it open. A wide-eyed jerk of her head told me it was my job to look into the room. Her eyes looked black in the red light.

'*Go on!*' she whispered angrily, fighting with the door to keep it open.

I knew I shouldn't; I knew that going in would be a mistake. My whole plan had been to avoid ever seeing that goblin again. If I didn't see it, sitting there on Gran's chest, it couldn't hurt her in real life. But for some reason, I couldn't stop myself.

I inched inside, half tripping on the rug.

'What do you see?' asked Cass.

The light in Gran's room was beyond feeble, but there was enough to see. Just. The goblin sat on her chest just like before – its knees and hips bent tight in a low squat. It sat there doing nothing, looking down at my gran's sleeping face. I pulled my head back.

'*It's the goblin.*' I mouthed it more than said it. My tongue felt sticky.

'How big is it?'

I shrugged a dunno. 'Like, dog-size? Maybe?'

'What sort of dog? Corgi? Great Dane?' Her eyes were big with frustration, so I ducked my head back inside the bedroom to get another look.

'You know, normal dog. Labradory.'

Cass seemed satisfied with that, and she whispered a final question. 'What's it doing?'

'Just sitting there.'

But it was like the goblin heard us – because right on cue, it leaned forward and started stroking Gran's face with the back of its long hand, the curled nails sliding smoothly across her forehead. Then it bent lower, as if it was about to kiss my gran's sleeping face. Swirls of blue-green light started drifting out of Gran's mouth, just like the night before.

'It's sucking green stuff out of her mouth,' I said.

'Jesus,' said Cass. 'It's a Maere!'

I turned back to look at her. Squid was squashed up against her, like a nervous puppy. 'Of course it's a night-mare. My whole life's been one bloody nightmare.'

'No,' said Cass, shaking her head. 'I don't mean it's a

71

bad dream. I mean it's a *Maere*. You know, as in the Maehr – the Maera?'

'I don't know what you're talking about.' I looked at Squid, hoping he could translate.

'I think she's talking about the old folklore.' Squid looked happier now he was explaining. He loves explaining stuff. 'The Maere was a demon who sat on your chest and sucked out your soul and gave you nightmares. It's where the word "nightmare" comes from. But they don't really exist.'

He finished with a smile, but it disappeared fast when Cass shoved him forward.

'This one does,' said Cass, as she pushed him into Gran's bedroom. She kept a firm grip on the back of his dressing gown so she could yank him out quick.

'Oh God,' he said quietly, and she pulled him back.

We stood there on the landing, looking at one another. Cass's face seemed angry. Or maybe just normal. I couldn't tell.

'Why didn't you say something before, idiot?' This was directed at me.

'Well, I'm sorry …'

I was still thinking of a witty comeback when she reached back over her shoulder and into a rucksack that I hadn't even noticed before. In the red gloom, I thought my eyes were confused because she seemed to pull out a frying pan. A big, heavy-bottomed, iron frying pan. She gave it a test swing and we both stepped back.

'Is that a frying pan?'

'It's a skillet,' she answered. 'OK, you two might need to get involved. Maeres can get nasty. And they learn quick too.' She waggled the pan. 'We need to do this fast and clean, OK?'

'Where'd you get the frying pan?' asked Squid. 'Can I get one?'

Cass took a deep, slow breath. She'd obviously had anger management classes at some point.

'Squid, you're in a dream,' she said quietly and slowly. 'You just have to believe it and you get it. D'you understand? Just … imagine it.'

Squid looked at her with a blank smile. The nappy-filling toddler was back. But while he stood there, smiling his awkward smile, I decided to believe her. *What have I got to lose?* I remember thinking, as I reached back over my shoulder into an imaginary rucksack.

The shock of feeling canvas fabric, and the sudden weight pressing down on my back, almost made me pull my hand away. But I didn't. I squeezed my eyes shut, forced myself to believe, and reached inside.

The frying pan I pulled out was substandard in many ways. Whereas Cass had something from the sixteenth century – all heavy iron and heft – mine looked like it was from a kid's playset. I shut my eyes again, forcing myself to believe it bigger, and just like that, it swelled heavier in my hand. When I opened my eyes the second time it was a normal, grown-up frying pan.

'That's non-stick,' said Squid, sounding pleased. I looked up to see he had a plastic spatula in his hand.

'Squid, we're not cooking.'

'I know. Sorry. My mind slipped. I was thinking about scrambled eggs.'

Now I looked, there was egg all over his spatula.

'OK, that's gonna have to do,' said Cass. 'I'll go in first. Don't come in unless I shout. But if I do shout, come quick. OK?'

And without another word she stepped into Gran's bedroom, and disappeared to black.

It was weird standing there. Waiting. Squid held up his little spatula like it was a dagger, and he didn't take his eyes off me for a second.

'What do you think she's going to do?' he whispered, but I could tell he didn't expect an answer.

We stood in silence for what felt like minutes, but was probably seconds. And then, one almighty clang later – the sound of iron on skull – Squid got his answer.

'Jeez, she must have bashed its brains right out of its head,' said Squid, his eyes big with fear and wonder.

I turned to go inside, suddenly annoyed with myself for leaving it all to Cass. But she was already back in the doorway.

'I'd leave it for five minutes,' she said firmly. My jaw must have dropped, because she laughed. 'I just mean, you don't want to have to clean that up in the morning, and if you see it – well, you know what might happen.'

The frying pan was still in her hand and she held it up like a trophy. Gently glowing blue-green slime oozed down the back of it.

'Is that goblin blood?' asked Squid from behind my shoulder, and Cass almost went cross-eyed looking at it.

'Well, I'm pretty sure it's brains, not blood,' she said.

And then she did something so unbelievable, so gross, it shouldn't even be in a nightmare. She stuck out her tongue and gave it a lick. Not a little testing, tasting lick, but a big fat lap of tongue like a cat with cream. Then she looked me right in the eye. 'And it's definitely a Maere, not a goblin. Which means you can kill it as many times as you like – but it will still be back tomorrow night.'

'OK,' said Squid. 'I think I've got some questions.'

But the siren on my phone alarm went off before he could even ask the first. And even though I suddenly wanted to stay, within a second, Squid, Cass, the whole world began to scramble, suddenly so fuzzy everything turned to grey noise – like it always does at the end of a dream.

I opened my eyes to the bright lamplight of my bedroom, and stayed awake until the sun came up.

10

WEDNESDAY

The next morning was Wednesday, and it was a horror show. Wednesdays are always a nightmare; the more traditional kind. We have four maths lessons. In a row. Yeah, you read that right. McCluskey sets the timetable. Double, double maths – you couldn't make it up.

But this Wednesday was the worst.

I must have fallen back asleep within about a minute of the sun coming up, because the next thing I remember was my gran shaking me awake. Her face looked worried, like she thought I might be dead.

'I thought you were dead,' she confirmed, and then pointed at the clock. 'It's gone nine o'clock, Finnegan, you're running late.'

Being late for school is always a misery. They make you go to the school office and sign a book and you have to give a reason. And 'I was in bed' isn't a reason, apparently.

Then, one of the 'Pastoral Care Team' comes and has 'a little chat' for the whole of first break, 'to see if there's anything we can do to help'. But there's always the unspoken threat that they'll send 'someone' round to your house. And they always ask about Gran, and how old she is. I hate that. Especially when they say things like, 'And how's your gran coping?' and 'Would you like someone to come round just to see if there's anything we can do to help?'

As you can imagine, I'm not late much.

Anyway, because of all that (and because he's in a higher set for maths) I didn't see Squid until lunch, so I had the whole morning to mull things over. And even with a foggy, sleep-starved brain, some things were becoming clear.

Cass was either a godsend who was going to save my gran and find my parents – or she was a total loose cannon who was going to destroy my life. At that point, I had no idea of the mess she was capable of making. If I had done, if I'd known what she was like, I'd have eaten my own eyelids rather than ever go to sleep again. But back then, on Wednesday – what are we talking, three days ago? Anyway, back then, just knowing that I wasn't the only one, knowing I wasn't on my own any more – in the dreams I mean – felt *good*.

Sitting there in double, double maths, doing algebra, I felt something that I hadn't felt in a long, long time: *optimism*. I doubt that's ever happened to anyone in double, double maths before.

I finally met up with Squid in the lunch queue and he was all smiles.

'So, buddy, are we on for tonight?' he said knowingly, then opened his school bag to reveal a stash of books. 'I've been doing some reading –' he switched to a loud whisper – 'and I think I've got a plan.'

Cass barged between us, biting on an apple. 'What's the plan, mini-man?' she said loudly, and Squid twitched. We were late for lunch and the dining hall was already half empty, but Squid clearly wasn't comfortable talking openly. He looked around the hall like a trainee spy, and then said quietly, 'I've got a way to kill the goblin. I mean, the Maere thing.'

Cass took another bite out of her apple, and then spoke through it. 'I told you. You can't kill a Maere, they just come back. The best you can do is move house – and hope they don't follow you.' She turned to me, shaking her head. 'But that never works.'

'So you said last night,' said Squid. He was using his 'smug professor' voice. The one he uses for explaining maths. No one likes the 'smug professor' voice. 'But there was something about that thing. I was sure I'd seen it before. And look.'

He pulled a small book from his bag – a burgundy hardback that fell open on some glossy illustration pages in the middle. He held the book towards me.

'Recognise anybody?'

It was an old oil painting, with a young woman, dramatically asleep – twisted like she was having a nightmare, curly, blonde hair spilling all over the place. She looked absolutely nothing like my gran. But on her chest sat a creature – its thick features fixed in a sneer. And that I did recognise.

'That's it. Exactly it.' I leaned forwards, almost hypnotised by it.

'But that painting must be, like, five hundred years old,' said Cass.

'Where's this book from?' I asked.

'Home,' said Squid. His mum has, like, a million books, so it wasn't a complete surprise.

Squid nodded quietly, and shut the book. 'Good, then we know what we're dealing with. From here on, this should be pretty straightforward.'

'You have no idea what you're talking about,' Cass butted in. She was helping herself to a plate of veggie korma and I instinctively found myself taking a step back.

'But the book says—' said Squid.

'I don't care what the book says. That … *thing* will just keep coming back – no matter what you do. And each time, it'll get smarter. Smarter than you and your book. And it's gonna get stronger, way stronger than anything I can handle. And it's …' She turned to me and paused. 'And it's got it in for you. Well, for your gran anyway. Once they start, these things don't leave till they've got *everything*.'

'What d'you mean, everything?' I managed to ask, not really wanting to hear the answer.

Cass pulled a face. I guess it was supposed to be a kind face, because she said: 'Sorry, but you need to know. They feed on souls.'

Now, I knew that. Deep down, I knew it was after my gran's brain, or mind or soul or whatever makes a human a human. But hearing it out loud just made my head flip. And my guts. It wasn't till we were sat down at a table that I could even trust myself to speak.

'So what's your plan, Squid?' I managed to ask.

He was already on the first bite of his cheeseburger,

81

so it was a bad time to ask, but he answered anyway. Squid's good like that.

'These nightmare goblin thingies. There are stories about them everywhere, literally everywhere. Every place on earth, all through history.'

He pulled out the burgundy book, and read out loud.

'In France they're called the *Cauchemar*, in Sweden the *Mara*. In the Dark Ages, the Germans called them *Alpen*.'

'What, as in the cereal?' asked Cass.

'Yeah. Well, no. But yeah, the same word. And they've been around forever. The Romans had something called an *incubus*. They even existed in Ancient Mesopotamia, like, five thousand years ago.'

'So these things aren't new,' I said.

'But that doesn't tell us anything we didn't know already,' said Cass. 'You don't understand. I've dealt with one of these things before. They don't stop, they just come back, night after night.'

She looked angry, so I didn't dare ask. Instead I said to Squid, 'So what *is* your plan?'

Squid had somehow managed to finish his cheeseburger, even though he'd been doing most of the talking. It's, like, his special power. Now he was on to his drink. He stopped sucking on the straw and took a deep breath before saying, 'All the stories say the same thing: the Maere can't be killed. You can't run from them, you can't trap them, you can't hide.'

'See?' said Cass. 'That's what I said.'

'All the stories except one.' Squid put down his carton of juice and wiped a hand on his trousers. Then he flipped to the back of the book, to the references.

'This book quotes from an old Latin manuscript.' He ran is his finger down the long list of footnotes, and stopped somewhere in the middle of the page. 'There it is, the *Malleus Maleficarum.*' He looked up, obviously pleased with himself. 'That basically means *The Hammer of Demons.*'

'Catchy,' I said, trying to lighten the tone. But Squid was on a roll.

'It was written by a German priest called Heinrich Kramer in the German city of Speyer in 1486. It's kind of like a *How-To Guide* for killing witches and demons.'

'And?' Cass looked genuinely interested for the first time.

'*And* I managed to find a copy online. I downloaded a translation on to my phone in the toilets.' He raised his eyebrows and looked down at his bag like there was a bomb in it.

'Let's see it then.'

'What?' Squid looked horrified. 'And have my phone confiscated? That's why I read it in the bogs.'

He was right. If you're caught using a phone, it's taken away for three days. Our school's worse than prison.

Cass let out a big, impatient breath. 'Well, tell us then.'

But Squid was enjoying this; he wasn't going to be hurried. He took another sip of juice before continuing. 'OK, so it tells the full story of how Heinrich banished demons with a bit of a – you know – ritual.'

'What, like an exorcism?' The contempt in Cass's voice actually made Squid flinch. But he managed to pull himself together.

'Yeah, something like that. But no, Heinrich calls it an *expulsion*. He did it loads. And it works.'

'Clever old Heinrich,' said Cass flatly. 'But I think I'll bring a skillet, just in case.'

Squid looked at me then. He was obviously aware that I'd hardly said a word since we'd sat down. 'So what's it gonna be, boss?'

'Boss?'

'Yeah, if I'm the brains and she's the muscle, there's only one job left – leader. And it is your gran. You should call the shots.'

I looked at Cass. 'Are you all right with that?'

'Sure, Boss Baby, whatever you say.'

Then the bell went, time for class.

'OK, let's do it,' I said, with a certainty I didn't feel. 'See you at mine tonight? Say, eleven o'clock?'

'Make it midnight,' said Cass.

11

MIDNIGHT

I spent the evening sketching. It's usually the one thing guaranteed to distract me from whatever it is I don't want to think about. But that night, all I could seem to draw were goblins. Even as I drew them, the faces gave me the creeps. But for some reason, I just couldn't stop.

Until midnight, when I turned down my light and settled in for sleep.

When my eyes opened, Squid was sitting on the end of my bed, which was weird.

'Dude, that's weird. How long have you been here?'

'About twenty minutes,' said Cass from the window sill. 'You're late.'

I looked at my watch. She was right.

'It takes me time to drop off, all right?'

'Then go to bed earlier.'

'But then I might …' I trailed off, because I was *about* to say: 'But then I might be on my own.' Which was totally lame.

'Well, we're all here now,' Squid interrupted my thoughts. 'No harm done.'

He had his school bag with him, bulging full, and I watched him unzip it and tip everything on to my bed.

'OK,' he said, picking up a pad and paper. 'Let's check we've got everything. First, prayer book.'

Cass looked bored. It was obviously my job to find everything.

'Is this it?' I said, holding up a white hardback titled *The Book of Common Prayer.*

'As long as you're not Catholic. If you are, use the blue one.'

I wasn't sure what I was, so I stuck with the white.

Squid looked back down at his list. 'Crucifix?'

'Check,' I answered. He'd brought a nice big chunky one. Metal.

'Sacred peanuts?'

'Peanuts?'

'Yep, the monkey nuts, I've … kind of blessed them.'

'You've *kind of blessed them?*' Cass stepped down from

the window sill and over to the bed. She picked up the bag of nuts and opened it. The monkey nuts were still in their shells.

'We haven't got many,' said Squid, stopping her arm before she could crack one open.

Cass smiled. 'OK, I get it. Don't eat the nuts till it's over.'

'And finally,' finished Squid, 'holy water.'

There was nothing on the bed, but when I picked up the bag it chucked out a drinks bottle on to the floor.

Cass picked up the bottle. 'I suppose you blessed this too?'

Squid shook his head, face serious. 'No, I stole that from the church.'

'Stolen holy water? Will that work?'

'Why wouldn't it?'

'I dunno. Maybe stealing holy water makes it a bit less … *holy*.'

'I hadn't thought of that.' Squid blinked and looked at me. 'What do you think?'

I looked at the bundle of rubbish Squid had brought to defeat an undefeatable goblin demon.

'This is nuts.'

'No, *these* are nuts.' Cass waved the bag of peanuts with a stupid grin, but Squid just ignored her.

'Look,' he said, pulling out his phone. 'We either trust the process, or we don't.' He scrolled down through the ebook he'd downloaded, of Heinrich Kramer's ancient manuscript.

'Heinrich sets it all out, the complete step-by-step. And we've got everything. Prayer book for incantations, crucifix for self-defence, holy water for emergencies, and a sacred object to, you know, trap the thing inside.'

'But they're peanuts.'

'It's one of the objects Heinrich recommends.' He showed us the screen. 'Look. Peanuts.'

It did say peanuts.

'It was either that or something even weirder, like a chicken or candles,' he said, scrolling down.

'Are you sure it's not a dodgy translation?' I said, but Cass had had enough.

'OK, you guys go with Heinrich. I'm gonna stick with a skillet. Let's go.'

'Use the skillet, and it will just come back tomorrow.' Squid stood up from the bed, facing Cass. He only came up to her chin, but I've never seen him looking so fierce. 'You said so yourself.'

Cass laughed, and it didn't help.

'And if we go in there on a peanut and prayer, then *we won't* be coming back tomorrow.'

They stood glaring at each other.

'I just don't think we should be trusting someone called Heinrich,' said Cass eventually.

'Well, that's a bit racist.'

'No it's not,' she snapped back.

'Yes it is – it's racist against Germans.'

'No it's not. It's just the name Heinrich. It's like Colin or Sebastian, or Timothy. I wouldn't trust them to do anything.'

'Well, then it's namist. It's still stereotyping.'

Squid had gone red in the face, Cass's jaw was clenched. This was going nowhere. Thankfully, at that moment, I remembered I was supposed to be the leader.

'OK, you two, we do both. Squid, us two will go in first and do the exorcism thingy. Cass only steps in if she needs to. OK?'

I sounded like a proper leader, and I was quite pleased with myself. For all of about three seconds. But then the banging started up.

Gran's bedroom door was off again. We listened to it bang maybe three or four times before Cass reached into her rucksack and pulled out the skillet. If anything, it looked bigger than the night before.

'So what, exactly, is the plan?'

'Yeah,' I agreed. 'How do we even do this, Squid?'

'It's simple. There are three steps.' He said it confidently, but then reached for his phone, which kind of ruined the effect. 'Step one is the *holding* phase. We use the crucifix to hold the demon in place. He can't come near us all the while you're holding it.'

'Then what?' said Cass.

Squid scrolled down, his face lit by the phone in the dim light. All the while Gran's door kept banging.

'Then,' he said, clearly struggling to find step two. 'It's the *verbal confrontation*. That's me, with the prayer book.' He scrolled again – down, then up, then down again. We watched in silence, painfully aware that Gran's door was banging itself off its hinges.

'Da-da-da, stuff about *risks* … *aftercare*, that's not it. Ah, here it is. *Entrapment*. We surround the Maere with the sacred objects, the peanuts.' Squid looked up to give me a pointed look. 'And then, reciting from the prayer book, we drive the spirit of the demon into the peanuts.'

'Into the peanuts?' I couldn't help repeating.

'Yes, into the peanuts.'

I could literally feel Cass trying not to say anything. But the door banged again and it broke her resolve.

'And then can we eat the peanuts?' she asked.

'I haven't read that far,' said Squid, putting the phone back in his bag. 'But I wouldn't think so.'

91

'So I'm on the crucifix?' I asked, picking it up for the first time.

'Yep, just use it like you would with a vampire. I'll do the rest.'

'Alrighty,' said Cass, clearly out of patience. 'Grab the gear, it's time for some *exorcise*.'

She said it with a grin, but no one laughed.

'I told you, it's not an exorcism,' said Squid. 'It's an expulsion.'

12

THE EXPULSION

We crept out on to the landing just like the night before. Cass went first, then me, Squid at the back. This time, Cass grabbed the swinging door with both hands and, with a nod, she beckoned us on.

I took a big belly breath, looked Squid in the eyes to make sure he was ready, and twisted the crucifix in my hand. It was metal, and reassuringly heavy. Worst case, I could use it as a weapon. He handed me the squeezy water bottle, and I suddenly realised I had no idea what to do with it.

'What do we do with the water?' I whispered, painfully aware that the goblin would be sitting, listening, on the other side of the open doorway.

'If the crucifix doesn't hold it, use the water.'

'Use it how?'

'I dunno. Squirt its face, maybe. Just don't waste it.'

I gave Cass a last look as she struggled to hold the door, and then inched into the bedroom. The crucifix was already sweaty in my hand. My heart was thumping now, and my eyes struggled to make patterns in the dark room.

I stepped through the doorway.

And just like before, there was the goblin, squatting happily on my sleeping gran. It was already smiling, like it had been waiting for me. Its head was even bigger than I remembered it. And then I saw why. It was wearing some sort of hat.

I didn't believe them at first, but the more my eyes adjusted, the clearer it got. The goblin creature was wearing a helmet – a crash helmet, like a racing driver from the old days, with stripes and a number.

'Oh wow!' said Squid's voice behind me. 'Lucky number seven.'

'What does that mean?' whispered Cass.

'I don't think it's lucky for us,' I said, not wanting to take my eyes off it. The metal crucifix felt hot in my sweaty hand, and slippery.

Squid bumped into my back and shunted me forward just as the creature turned to Gran. Its long fingers reached towards her, and with a cry I held up the crucifix.

I don't quite know what I was expecting. In horror movies the vampire generally kind of clutches itself in agony. As if all that holiness is just too painful. But the goblin didn't even seem to notice. It reached forward, stroked my gran's forehead with those talony fingers, and then leaned down with its mouth.

Something inside me snapped. And I threw the crucifix.

I was in the Year 7 softball team last term, so I can throw. And there was something about the weight and balance of the cross that made it easy to aim. The cross spun as it sliced through the air – and then right into the goblin's helmet.

You know how people always talk about things going through things like a hot knife through butter? Well, this was more like a fire hose *blasting* through butter. The top of the goblin's head literally exploded.

I shut my eyes and felt *stuff* splatter on to my face. But when I opened them, the goblin was still there, smiling at me, its helmeted head half gone.

'Oh no,' said Squid behind me. And then started reading from the book.

'*I command thee, unclean spirit, in the name of Anu,*

and in the name of Ishtar –' he spoke fast, tripping over the words – *'that thou come out and depart.'*

And so it went on. If anything, the goblin seemed to be enjoying itself. First it listened, then twisted its body, slowly clambering off my gran's chest and down on to the thick rug. And then it crawled, slowly, on all fours. Like a baby, but with half a head.

Squid was talking so fast now, the words were just a blur. And I couldn't help thinking, as the goblin inched closer, that maybe his words were too mumbled to work.

I looked down, helpless in horror, into the empty bowl of the goblin's half-exploded skull. It was like a walnut shell – without the walnut. The goblin reached towards me with that long, bony hand – and, with a gentle tap, touched the top of my bare foot with the point of its fingernail.

The jolt up my leg was like a bolt of electricity, right up and into my chest – the power seemed to fill my heart. The force of it was terrible, like the muscle of my heart wanted to wrench itself apart. My whole body stiffened, maybe from the surge of energy, or maybe just in terror.

And then, worst of all, everything began to tighten. It felt like a giant hand had been shoved down my throat and into my chest. There's no other way of describing it:

a giant hand grabbing my heart, and forcing it smaller and smaller, clenching down until I could feel the veins and vessels squashed to bursting.

'Use the water, you putz!' Cass's voice was muffled, and I barely heard the words. I could tell she was shouting, but it was like she was shouting from far away, or the bottom of a swimming pool. I heard her, but I didn't understand. I couldn't understand, not with that clamp around my heart. I couldn't even see, let alone think.

But some instinct or reflex made me squeeze the plastic bottle. I felt water run cold on to my hand as it spilt down the sides. And then cool drops as they landed on my bare foot. I looked down, but I still couldn't see. The whole world seemed to shudder, and for a moment I thought I'd fall. Then somebody – Cass – shoved past me and I did fall.

The sound of Cass's frying pan smacking into what was left of the Goblin's crash helmet was like a gunshot. The grip on my heart began to loosen and, gasping for air, my eyesight returned in a single beat of my heart. I looked up to see Cass smiling, offering me a hand.

'Told you we should stick with the skillet,' she said. 'Look, I smashed it right through the window.'

I saw in horror that she'd obliterated my gran's

bedroom. The old leaded windows were bent and smashed open. Half the wall missing, Gran's window seat totally gone.

'Gran loves that window seat,' I said pathetically, looking out on to the patio below, fresh air on my face. The goblin had made a dent in the lawn – it lay there, stunned but still smiling. Like it was having a happy dream.

'Is it dead?' said Squid, trying to peer over my shoulder. 'I didn't finish the incantation.'

'Come on – let's finish this,' said Cass, leaping out the smashed window.

For a moment I just watched her in surprise. I'd almost forgotten this was a dream. I jumped carefully, landing gently beside her.

'It's still alive,' Cass shouted up to Squid. 'Finish it.'

I think we both expected Squid to jump down, but he didn't. He stood by the smashed open wall and read from the book, standing over us like a preacher in a pulpit.

'... *And presume not to tyranny.*' Squid tossed peanuts as he read. They scattered down, and for the first time, the goblin's expression changed. The smile disappeared.

'*May Aku bestow the power ...*' said Squid, now slower,

and louder. As he said the final words, his voice was almost calm. '*In the union of Spirit, of Anu and Ishtar, world without end. Amun.*'

And then the strangest thing: the goblin began to fizz, like a bath bomb in water. Juddering and dissolving as if the air itself were acid.

'This is gonna be gross,' said Cass. And the fizzing goblin gave us a last, uncertain smile.

And then, like a prize idiot, I shut my eyes. I shut my eyes just before it exploded.

At least, I think it exploded. In fact, I'm 99.9 per cent *sure* it did, because I heard it explode, and I felt it. Goblin juice raining down on to my face and body. I imagined it exploding like a pricked water bomb, and when I opened my eyes there were thick puddles of slime all over the patio and lawn.

But when I think back, I don't think about the 99.9 per cent certainty, I think about the 0.1 per cent doubt. Because unless you see something happen, right then and there with your own eyes, you can never be totally certain. At the time, it never occurred to me how important that 0.1 per cent would turn out to be. I was too busy wiping goblin juice off my face.

I looked up at Squid; he was leaning out the smashed-open window, wide-eyed and covered in brick dust.

'What now?' I asked.

'Look at the peanut,' he answered, pointing. And we all watched as the goblin goo rivered towards one of the peanuts.

It began to spin, as if the goblin juice were giving it a life force of its own. And the more liquid it sucked up, the faster it spun. We watched it absorb every drop, and only then did it start to slow, coming to a halt at the edge of the patio, nestled against some grass.

'What do we do now?' I asked, not really expecting an answer.

'I think we need to keep that peanut somewhere safe,' said Cass, picking it up carefully. 'Somewhere *very* safe.'

'But what about the window?' I looked up at the room. It wasn't just the window; half the wall had been smashed away. Squid stood there nervously, clearly worried he might fall. 'If I wake up now, we might need a new house.'

'Then don't wake up now,' said Cass, still looking at the peanut. 'Fix it.'

'How do I do that?' I said, more in despair than anger.

'How many times do I need to say it? It's a dream, genius. Dream it fixed.'

I must have looked blank, because she sighed in irritation.

'Look, shut your eyes and remember what it used to look like.'

I started to speak, but she gave me a look.

'Just do it.'

I shut my eyes.

'Squid, you too!' she shouted up at him. 'Shut your eyes and remember what it used to look like – on the inside. Keep thinking of that. And *believe* it.'

I heard her take a big breath, and then another.

'How can this possibly work?' I said, and immediately regretted it.

'Just shut up and keep your eyes closed. You need to understand this place – this plane of existence. It's like a parallel universe to our own. It looks pretty much identical because we create it, all of us, when we dream. That's why everything is usually where you expect it – your house, your street, town, school, everything. Except, things can get … twisted.'

'What do you mean, twisted?'

I opened my eyes and saw that hers were now shut. She looked younger with her eyes shut. Less fierce.

'You know, twisted-distorted,' she said, frowning. 'All those weird little things that are different in dreams. In the dreamworld things get twisted because everyone can change things, just by thinking them and believing them. That's why you can fly in a dream – you can fight, jump over a house, anything.'

'That doesn't make sense. It can't be like that. It wouldn't work.'

'Why not?'

'Well, what happens if I jump off a cliff, thinking I can fly – but somebody else thinks I can't. Who wins?'

'What do you mean, *who wins*?'

'I mean, do I fly? Or do I *not* fly? When you jump off a cliff, there's a big difference.'

'Well, it depends. On who wants it most. Who believes it most.'

'So it all comes down to who has the most faith?'

'Pretty much. But also …' She hesitated for a moment, bit her lip – clearly struggling to decide whether to continue. Eventually, with a breath, she did. 'It also depends on *who* is doing the believing. Some people are special. They can believe more powerfully than others. That's why their dreams sometimes cross over – back into reality.'

'You mean me? You're saying I'm … special?' I said, grinning.

'In your dreams.' She smiled at her choice of words. 'At least, my dad thinks so. He called you a superhero – can you believe that?'

'Do you believe it?' I said, smiling back. It was somehow easier talking to her like this, when she had her eyes shut. There was less to think about.

'Let's say, I'm still making my mind up,' she answered.

'So what happens if I decide we can't fix that window?'

'Do you really believe that?' she said, smiling, her eyes still shut.

'No,' I admitted.

'Good, then open your eyes, because you're right not to.'

She opened her eyes then, and looked at me, still smiling. Then together we looked up at the cottage.

'See? All fixed.'

And it was. Everything was back. The wall, the window, everything. Even the rubble on the lawn was gone. I could see Squid – smiling, eyes still shut – but now on the other side of the leaded windows.

I shouted up at him, but he couldn't hear. So I ran inside and up to the bedroom.

'Squid,' I said softly. 'You can open your eyes. We did it, buddy, it worked. Heinrich one, Goblin nil. You can go back to bed now.'

I don't know if I dreamed any more after that. I certainly don't remember anything. But I woke at about four

103

o'clock in the morning, like I often do. And I struggled to get back to sleep, like I always do.

All in all, *Goblin Dream 3* had given me a lot to think about.

First up, that goblin *touch*.

I've always been so terrified of the things in dreams. The monsters. So scared, I've never let them get anywhere near me. But never, even in my wildest nightmares, did I ever think it would be that bad. The feel of that invisible hand gripping my heart, squeezing the blood out of it, trying to burst it, was so much worse than *anyone* could imagine.

'Never again,' I whispered to myself. I would never again let one of those creatures touch me, ever. No matter what it took.

But mostly, I thought about Cass and what she'd said. At the end.

It's like a parallel universe to our own. It looks pretty much identical because we create it, all of us, when we dream. Except, things can get … twisted.

Could that be true?

Squid will know, I eventually decided, and fell asleep just before my alarm went off.

13

THURSDAY

On Thursday I woke early, but happy.

We'd done it. Destroyed it. The goblin, the Maere, whatever it was called, was gone. For the first time in forever, I could see a way out. Light at the end of the tunnel that was my miserable life. I lay on the bed, smiling at the ceiling. My living nightmare might just be coming to an end.

I even dared think about Mum and Dad. Could we really find them? Cass seemed sure of it. But then I thought of the zombies, and the woman with no eyes. And without even meaning to, I was suddenly up and getting dressed. Anything to shake off that memory.

I'd have given a lot to go back to sleep; I was knackered, even by my standards. But there was no way I was going to be late two days in a row – it would pretty much guarantee a home visit. So, after checking in on a sleeping Gran, I skipped breakfast and cycled into school early.

Squid's mum drops him off on the way to work, and he was already at the gates when I parked up. He was pretty hyped, but I managed to calm him down enough to ask him about Cass's theory.

'A parallel universe created by our brains? Why not? Sounds as good a theory as any,' he said non-committally. 'Some physicists even think *this* universe is just a creation of our brains.'

'What?'

Squid laughed. 'They think this reality – time, space, everything – is created by the minds of the people observing it.'

'What does that even mean?'

'OK, try thinking about this: if a tree falls in a forest and no one's around to hear it, does it make a sound?'

'Yes,' I said. 'Obviously.'

'How do you know?'

'Because trees make a noise when they fall over.'

'You don't know that.'

'Yes. I do.'

'No you don't. You only know that the trees *you've heard fall over* make a noise.'

'But I've never heard a tree fall over.'

'Then how do you know they make a noise?'

'It's just obvious.'

'I guess you should let the physicists know you've got it all figured out then.'

I could tell he was laughing at me, but I was determined not to let it go.

'So you're saying there are scientists, real scientists, who believe that what Cass said is true?'

'Yeah, sure. At least, they think it *could* be true. But there's no way of testing it, so what's the point.'

A funny thing happened to Squid's face then. His lips started twitching like he was about to say something, but nothing came out. Like he was mumbling underwater. Then his face broke into a smile. He looked at me as though he were seeing me for the first time in his life.

'Except now we can.' His eyes were glistening and his voice was suddenly loud. '*You* have the power to change the world.'

I looked around, worried the other kids would look up from their phones. But they didn't.

'How?' I whispered, deliberately quiet.

'Because *your* dreams change the world. You said so yourself. Just dream something really cool.'

'Like what?'

'I don't know. Dream me up a Ferrari.'

'You can't drive.'

'Then dream up a chauffeur.'

'This is ridiculous,' I said, as the bell rang and the gates opened.

Thursday mornings aren't much better than Wednesdays. Second lesson is geography and it's with McCluskey. It's just about the worst lesson of the week, mainly because he always picks on me. McCluskey's got a sixth sense for knowing what I don't know – which, to be fair to him, is just about all of it.

Anyway, he's got this 100 per cent hit rate for firing questions that are guaranteed to humiliate me. And by Thursday, I was so tired I could barely stay awake – let alone pay attention to what McCluskey was droning on about.

To make it worse, near the end of the lesson, Sully, my personal bully and arch-nemesis, came into the classroom. He was escorting a bunch of prospective parents on a school tour. It's exactly the sort of thing Sully volunteers for. He's such a crawler.

McCluskey saw the chance for maximum humiliation, and sure enough, as soon as the chance came up –

'Finnegan Quick, name a greenhouse gas that *isn't* carbon dioxide.'

I've looked it up since. I now know the answer is methane, CH_4, one carbon atom plus four hydrogen. But at the time all I could remember was it had something to do with cow farts.

McCluskey looked at me with his usual 'bewildered disappointment', so I gave him the best answer I could.

'Farts? Sir.'

Everyone laughed. McCluskey chewed his cheek. He obviously thought I was mucking about, and I thought he was going to start shouting. But he didn't, not with all those future parents standing there.

That's when I saw the woman. The woman without eyes. She stood at the back of the group, absurdly out of place for a school tour, her bandaged eyes facing me, unseeing. No one else seemed to notice.

I turned back to McCluskey. Surely he would say something? But he wouldn't take his eyes off me. Just kept staring, chewing the side of his mouth. The class went deathly quiet and you could hear his teeth grinding on the meat of his cheek – like he was chewing through it again. And then I realised: he was.

'Oh, that's gross,' said a girl's voice from behind me. And then the whole class was talking and pointing and shouting. Because McCluskey kept chewing, grinding away like a dog with a bone. And then the black beetle was back; long jaws poking through the bloody flaps of McCluskey's cheek.

Someone screamed. Lots of people screamed. Maybe even me.

This time, after taking a good look around, the bug unfolded its wings and threw itself into the air. It thrummed across the room, barely able to carry its enormous weight. Most ducked, everyone silent. I sat transfixed as it landed right on Sully's face, and his smug, self-satisfied smile disappeared.

Sully's eyes crossed comically as he tried to focus on the beetle, now sitting on the bridge of his nose. And they widened in alarm as the beetle started crawling, collapsing itself small to enter one of his nostrils.

We all sat hushed, watching. For a few seconds nothing happened, and then one of his eyes, the left I think, started to twitch. The eyelid fluttered and the eyeball juddered horribly. It went red, as if a vein had burst. And then it went black. As if the beetle had worked its way into the eye socket and started to feast.

'It's eating his eyeball!' someone screamed.

Now, you know I hate Sully. Probably more than anyone else on the planet. He's made my life a misery from the day I joined this school. But as his eyeball was slowly hollowed out, even I started to shout for help.

'It's just a dream,' said a voice.

At first, I thought it was the voice in my head, and I immediately knew it was right; this wasn't real – I had to wake up.

'Finn, mate, wake up. It's just a dream.' This time I recognised the voice and opened my eyes to see Squid standing above me.

Reality slapped me between the eyes and I reared backwards, tipping off my chair. There was dribble down my chin and I looked around from the floor, wide-eyed, to see a classroom of kids all gawping at me. They were smiling, then laughing. I'd obviously put on quite a show.

Sully was there too – with a bunch of prospective parents. They hustled their terrified kids out into the corridor.

'Thank you, Finnegan,' said McCluskey's voice over the chatter. 'If you could leave the freak show at home next lesson, I'd be very grateful.' He got a laugh for that, the jerk.

For the rest of the lesson I just tried to make myself invisible. And when the bell finally went, I sat there, waiting for everyone to leave before I did. But the smiles told me I was never going to be allowed to forget.

'Nice one, *Freak Show Finn*,' said someone, cuffing

me round the back of the head on their way out. I didn't even look up to see who.

'Did I shout out and stuff?' I asked Squid nervously, when everyone had gone.

'Don't worry about it,' he said, which meant yes, I had. That sort of humiliation lasts a lifetime.

We went straight to the field at break. There's an old oak tree where we usually hang out, right at the far end of the field, by the fence. It's kind of reassuring to know you're only one climb away from freedom. But we mainly go there because people leave us alone; no one else can be bothered to go that far.

So it was a bit surprising to see Cass there, leaning against the tree.

'Here, this is for you.' She tossed something at Squid, but he dropped it.

We both looked down to see the peanut from the night before.

'Well, pick it up then,' said Cass.

'You pick it up,' said Squid. He seemed different today. Bolder.

'OK, whatever, let the squirrels have it for all I care. I just thought Heinrich would have something to say about what to do with it.'

'I told you.' Squid shrugged. 'I didn't read that far.'

We all backed away from the peanut in unspoken agreement. It could rot in the ground for all I cared.

'What happened?' said Squid. 'I thought you were going to eat it. Lose your nerve?'

Cass grunted. And then we all watched dumbfounded as a squirrel ran down the tree and across to the nut. It picked it up with both paws, looked at us, then scampered through the metal railings and into the field beyond.

'That's just great, guys,' I said. 'Well done. Now you've unleashed a demon squirrel.'

'What's grumping him out?' said Cass.

'He fell asleep in class, and kind of got a bit ... shouty.' Squid looked at me, and pulled an apologetic face.

'That's awkward,' said Cass. 'What was the dream about?'

'You don't wanna know,' I said automatically.

'Yeah, I wanna know. What was it about?'

'None of your business.' I'd had enough of people traipsing through my dreams like they were public property.

'Yes, it is my business. *You* are my business. I'm here to find your mum and dad, remember? Besides, I saved your gran last night. You owe me.'

'Well, then *you* owe *us* … some answers.'

'Answers to what?'

'To our questions, and none of this *There's only time for three questions* bull.' I was angry and not in the mood to hide it. 'We want to know everything. Why you're *really* here. How you know about my mum and dad. *Who even are you?*'

I looked at Squid for support.

'It *would* be nice to know a bit more about you. And your dad,' he said feebly.

Cass let out a breath and gave me the sort of look teenagers usually save for their parents.

'Look, I told you. My dad's a paranormal investigator.'

'No one does that. It's not a real job,' I snapped back.

'Well, he's been doing it for twenty years – so I guess yes, it is, actually.' Cass stared at me angrily, but I wasn't going to back down.

'But could you tell us a bit more?' said Squid. 'You seem to know everything. And we're totally … clueless.'

Cass looked at Squid, then back at me. All the while blowing out her cheeks. Eventually she slumped back on to the tree.

'Look, my dad's a researcher – into all sorts of weirdo,

paranormal, supernatural stuff. He's a proper scientist, at a university. So yes, it is his job. His real specialty is cases like you.'

'What do you mean, cases like me?'

'You know, dream-reality entanglement. Where bits of dreams bleed over into real life. I told you. It happens. Not often, and hardly ever this extreme. But it happens.'

'How *hardly ever*?' I crossed my arms, determined to get full answers. 'In the twenty years your dad's been investigating this "weird stuff", how often has he come across a case as extreme as mine?'

'Like, maybe twice. Including you. I told you, my … mum was like it too.'

'Your mum, who died?' Her face kind of collapsed when I said that, and I couldn't help feeling like a jerk.

She swallowed before speaking again, and for a second I thought she might cry. But she didn't. Instead she said, 'Now your turn. Tell me about the dream.'

'I saw the woman again,' I said simply.

'What woman?'

'You know what woman – the one from the crypt, with no eyes. She was in class, on a school tour.'

Cass's face stiffened.

'Yeah, exactly,' I said, still not sure I wanted to tell her everything. Or Squid either. I'd never told anyone about the woman before. About what she'd done to my dog, Biscuit. And Mum and Dad. It might sound stupid, but telling people felt somehow disloyal to their memory. Like I was giving away someone else's secrets.

'There's something I didn't tell you,' I said eventually. 'I've seen her before. She was there when my dog disappeared. I think she's always been there – in my dreams, I mean. When something really bad happens, she's always there.'

Cass nodded.

'Don't you have anything to say?'

'Why would I?'

God, she could be infuriating.

'When you saw her,' I said very deliberately, 'in the crypt … you screamed. And you never scream.'

'So?'

'So my question is, why? Why did you scream?'

Cass looked at Squid, then back at me. She seemed to think for a long time.

'All right,' she said eventually. 'Come to mine, tonight, both of you. I'll explain everything. You can see my dad.'

Squid and I looked at each other.

'Do you mean really come? Or dream it?'

'No, you idiots, there's a lot you need to see. Come and sleep over.'

We must have both looked terrified because she laughed.

'No need to freak out. What, have you never had a sleepover at a girl's house before?'

She laughed louder, clearly knowing the answer, and with a sudden jump was pulling herself up into the branches of the tree. She hooked a leg over and in one fluid movement twisted herself up on to the branch. A moment later she was sitting comfortably, looking down on us.

'Come round about seven, give yourself plenty of time before it gets dark,' she said, and was suddenly up on her feet, walking the length of the branch like a gymnast on a beam, out and beyond the spiked metal fence.

We knew she'd nail the landing, even before she'd jumped. She moved like gravity was for other people.

'Wait, are you going?' I said stupidly. 'It's only first break.'

'I think I'm done for the day.' She turned along the footpath that runs parallel to the school fence.

'But we don't even know where you live,' I shouted after her.

'Yeah, you do,' she said without looking back. 'My dad bought the old manor. You know, Freak House.'

It's safe to say that the rest of the school day dragged.

Really dragged. Most school days run at half speed, but this was more like torture. French, history, geography, they just piled up in a blur of endless blah. Facts and figures and 'things you need to know for the exam', all pummelling my brain like a fist of boredom.

All I could think about was spending the night at Freak House with Cass. Even lunchtime dragged. Squid had a flute lesson, so I spent most of it on my own.

And then, on the way back to class, I bumped into Sully. Literally bumped into him. He was coming in from the soccer pitch; they must have had a game because he and his mates were in full kit, boots and everything. He shoulder-barged me, and I fell right on my backside.

I don't know the last time you did that, but if you land on the bony bit of your bum, it really hurts. Like, pain-all-up-your-back hurts.

'What the hell?' I said automatically.

And then I wished I hadn't.

Sully was standing over me. He's tall, *really* tall in studs. And despite being a total-suck-up dweeb, he does a lot of sport. And he looks, well, a lot bigger than me at the best of times. Now, towering over me, he looked massive.

There was something different about him too. And

then he blinked and the pain in my butt disappeared, as a surge of adrenalin gushed into my blood. Because Sully's eyes ... had gone completely black.

He looked left, then right, and then up to double-check for CCTV cameras (I told you it was a rough school). And I knew exactly what was coming next: he was going to stick the boot in.

I tried to scramble back, but he raised his studs, ready to break my leg. I could almost feel the pain, hear the crack of shattering bone.

But instead I heard music. Flute music.

It came from inside the school, and then burst through the double doors. It was Squid, and he was *dancing* too. A little pirate jig, or maybe a Cossack dance or something. It was hard to tell. But he kept spinning and prancing about as he played.

You can imagine, phones were out in a heartbeat. But still, *he just kept dancing*. And with little head shakes, and smiles and raised eyebrows. Absolute humiliation. The stuff of nightmares.

It only ended when he reached Sully. With a final, violent tap dance, he blew a high-pitched chord, right in Sully's face.

There was silence, everyone thinking the same as me. Sully would crush Squid like a little bug. He was twice his size. But Sully just stood there, staring down at Squid. Squid smiled, spit dripping from the end of his flute.

And then? Well, then Sully just walked away.

The cheers and the applause would have been heard on the other side of the school. Squid took a bow, then more, and after waving and punching the air, he leaned down to help me to my feet.

'Mate?' I said, struggling to stand. 'What was that?'

'It was Bach. Sonata in B minor.'

'No, I don't mean what was the music. I mean, what *was* that? The dance and everything. You know people got it on video.'

Getting a video of someone dance-fighting with a flute was definitely worth losing your phone for – even for three days. And I'd seen half a dozen phones out, minimum.

'Oh, it's just a mind trick. *Irrational behaviour strategy*. You use it to get out of a fight.' Squid was putting his flute back in its case. He didn't seem to realise the magnitude of what he'd just done. 'You just do something so weird that you kind of pull the rug out from under whoever it is who wants a fight. You should try it, it's totally foolproof.'

'Thanks, mate,' was all I could think to say. It was

pretty pathetic thanks compared to what he'd done. Squid, as I've said a few times now, never ceases to amaze me.

'I wish you were coming tonight,' I said, when we were back in the classroom, waiting for afternoon register.

'What do you mean? Of course I'm coming tonight.'

'But what about your mum?' After Tuesday's detention his mum would be on the warpath.

'Leave her to me.'

'You know, you don't have to. This is my mess. I can sort it.'

Squid smiled. 'I would normally agree with you. But ...'

'But what?'

Squid seemed to hesitate. He looked uneasy, but eventually he said, 'You know last term, I showed you how to tell if someone's lying?'

'Yeah?' I had the strong feeling I didn't want to hear what Squid was about to say next.

'Well, it's Cass.' Squid rubbed his eyes, and then looked right at me. 'She's not telling us the truth. She's hiding something. About her dad, and Freak House.'

14

SLEEPOVER AT FREAK HOUSE

My first thought as they took afternoon register was a coward's thought: Squid's mum would never let him sleep over in a million years. Not on a school night. Especially after Tuesday's detention. That meant it would just be me going to Freak House. Sometimes life's easier having strict parents – they're the perfect excuse.

Squid seemed convinced he could persuade her, but for the rest of the day I couldn't helping worrying. God knows what Cass's dad would be like. A total monster probably, to have produced something as snarky as Cass. But I should've trusted Squid. Because at 6.45 p.m., on the dot, he knocked on my door.

He wanted to come in, but Gran had been acting a

bit strange – watching TV all afternoon, but with her hearing aid out, so she couldn't even hear it. Or me. And for some reason, I didn't want Squid to see her like that. He'd ask questions I couldn't answer. So instead we went straight on to Cass's.

We walked most of the way in silence, but as we crunched up the long gravel drive, I couldn't help asking, 'Please tell me you didn't pack your Spider-Man pjs?'

'What's wrong with Spider-Man pjs?' he said, but smiled to reassure me he was joking. At least, I think so; with Squid you're never quite sure.

Even from a distance the house looked creepy. It's hard to say why, exactly. The grim old church behind it didn't help. But it's not like it was painted with blood or anything. It was just a *heavy*-looking house, all shadows and grey stone and steep roofs with long old chimneys that looked ready to topple over and kill you. Some of the windows were boarded up with bits of old timber, but even that wasn't it, exactly.

'I can see why they call it Freak House,' said Squid, halfway up the drive. 'Those black stains running down the stone make it look like it's bleeding.' He stopped walking and I stopped too, both of us staring at the house.

123

'You know how some houses look like cute faces, with windows as eyes and doors as a nose?' he said quietly. 'Well, this one looks like it's dying.'

'Thanks, mate, and there I was, really looking forward to tonight.'

There's no doorbell on a place like that, just a cold metal ring on a chain. Squid gave it a tug and the sound of a bell echoed somewhere deep inside.

Cass answered the door surprisingly quickly. She looked about, as if checking we weren't being followed, and then beckoned us inside, to an empty hallway. I was immediately struck by how cold it was.

'What were you looking for?' I said. 'Out there, I mean.'

'Just, you know, crows,' said Cass vaguely. 'Come on, this hallway always gives me the creeps. Let's go through.'

We went down a passage to the left, and eventually into a big, old-fashioned kitchen. The sort you'd expect to see filled with a cook and servants. There was a mattress on the tiled floor.

'This is where we'll sleep. Don't worry, I've got more mattresses,' she said, opening a big, surprisingly new fridge.

'What about the bedrooms?'

'Oh, you don't want to go upstairs. Trust me. This place used to be a care home. It's pretty grim up there.'

'What d'you mean?' said Squid, speaking for the first time since we'd arrived.

'Well, when I say care home, I mean *psychiatric* care. And when I say *care*, I'm not sure there was much of that. I think they used to just lock them in their rooms.'

'There are locks on the bedrooms?' said Squid.

'Yeah, and they lock from the outside. Inside there are drawings, all over the walls. It's all a bit, you know – nightmare fuel.' She looked at me and repeated, 'Trust me, you don't want to go upstairs. Drink? I got juice, fizzy water, tap water, different juice.'

'I'm good,' I said. Squid just shook his head. Cass shrugged and helped herself to a bottle from the fridge.

'I don't mean to be rude,' I continued, 'but why here? I mean, why *this* house?'

'It's horrible,' Squid blurted out, and Cass laughed awkwardly.

'That's gonna take some explaining,' she said. 'Come on, follow me.'

There must have been four doors coming off the kitchen. Cass picked one and led us into another hallway and then an empty room. There was furniture, but not much, and it was all covered in sheets. Squid gave me the raised eyebrows, but Cass kept walking.

I'd known this night wasn't going to be completely normal, but this place was off the charts. Cass looked nervous, for one thing. And even in the short time I'd known her, that was never a good sign.

'Where is your dad?'

'In his study,' she said, not looking at me. 'But he can wait. I need to show you some stuff first. Come on.'

After that, we passed through a couple more rooms just like it. Any furniture was covered, but there wasn't much. It felt like we were working our way to the back of the house, but by the time she stopped, in another hallway, outside two big double doors, I was already lost. This hall had its own stairway, spiralling up the wall. And I remember thinking how weird it must be to live in a house so big there was more than one set of stairs.

'OK,' said Cass, inviting us through the double doors and smiling for the first time. 'This is the library. *This* is where you'll get some answers.'

She opened the doors on to a giant room, and we stepped inside. This room, at least, was lived in. Old leather armchairs huddled round a huge fireplace, which lit up the near wall with a warm yellow flame. In

126

the middle of the room was a big oval table, covered in stacks of paper and piles of green folders, most of them tied with red ribbon. But it was the far wall that really caught your eye: a huge bay window, broad enough to fill the entire wall, the small panels and glass doors looking out on to a terrace. Beyond that was a neat lawn which ended with an old brick wall. And behind that was the church.

And the graveyard, I thought to myself.

There was a wooden door set into the brick wall that marked the boundary between the garden and the churchyard. I wondered if they kept it locked. I know I would.

'Where are the books?' said Squid, and I noticed the empty shelves for the first time. The walls were covered in them, from floor to ceiling, but there wasn't a single book anywhere.

'Probably went mouldy,' said Cass. 'If you think the place is bad now, you should have seen it two months ago when we moved in.'

'Is this your dad's study?' I said, looking at all the files stacked up on the oval table. I was trying to bring the subject back round to her father. There was something weird about the way she didn't want to talk about him.

'No, his study's through there,' she said, nodding at

the far door. It was newly painted glossy white, and firmly shut. She looked out on to the garden through the big windows. 'You'll see him soon, I promise.'

Then she turned to us with a big smile and said, 'OK. So you got questions.'

'Why are you here?' Squid fired out the first.

'My dad bought this place back in May. And we moved here in July—'

'But why?' I interrupted.

'I told you. He was investigating your mum and dad.'

'But why here?'

'I think you know why.' Cass sat on the arm of a chair and finally looked me in the eye. 'Because it's next to the cemetery. And the crypt. Where your mum and d—'

'How do you know *anything about* my mum and dad?'

'I told you that too. We investigate anomalies. Paranormal anomalies. And also …' Cass paused while she looked from me to Squid and then back at me. 'Also because he was looking for *my* mum.'

'You said she died – when you were a little kid,' I couldn't help firing back.

'She did …' Cass hesitated again. 'But she's never really, you know, gone away. Not completely.'

Squid gave me a look and Cass saw it.

'OK, you two, sit down and I'll tell you everything.

Just shut up with the questions, all right? I'll answer them at the end.'

We sat in the armchairs by the fire and Squid gave it a good prod with an iron poker.

'Right, it goes like this. You've probably never heard of my mum, but when she was alive, she was a big deal. She was, like, rich. Really rich.'

'What was her name?' said Squid.

'Mallory. Mallory McAllaster.'

He blinked. 'You're right. I have never heard of her. I didn't even know that was a name.'

'Anyway,' Cass continued, '*her* parents, my grandparents, died when she was a little kid, but even so, when Dad met her, she'd already made a ton of money. We don't really know where from.'

'How did your dad meet her?' asked Squid, still poking at the fire.

I thought Cass was going to tell him to shut up and listen, but she didn't.

'Dad was already doing paranormal research at that point—'

'Into this ... dream-reality entanglement?' interrupted Squid again.

'Yeah, and other stuff. Weird stuff. Look, will you just shut up and listen? Mum just happened to be one of his first study subjects.' Cass downed a big slug of juice, then looked right at me. 'She could change the world, like you. Dad said that if she wanted something to happen, she could just dream it into existence.'

'Is that how she got to be so rich?' said Squid, obviously still thinking about his Ferrari.

'I guess so. She certainly had everything you ever dream of. She had millions, billions probably. And she and Dad, well, they fell in love, had a beautiful baby girl and lived happily ever after, for about a year and a half.'

'When she died?' I couldn't help asking.

'Yes. On the morning of June thirteenth. A car crash, on the way to the office. The paramedics put the time of death as thirteen minutes past five.'

I must have gone red or looked a bit antsy, or both, because Squid looked at me and said, 'What?'

'That date, the thirteenth of June, when Cass was a one-year-old … don't you get it?'

Squid made a face.

'It's my birthday, you numpt. The actual day I was born.'

'And not just the day,' said Cass. She stood and went over to the big oval table in the middle of the room. She thumbed down a tall stack of green folders, before sliding one out.

'My dad has a theory. That whatever power, or gift, or curse my mum had … gets passed on … at the precise moment of death.'

'What, like the Dalai Lama?'

We both turned to Squid. 'What do you mean?' I asked.

'Well, you know, the Dalai Lama, the Tibetan monk guy. He keeps being reincarnated, so every time one dies they have to look for the next one.'

'What, like a little mini-baby Dalai Lama?' I asked, unable to stop myself smiling. I'm always amazed at the stuff Squid knows.

'Exactly, they're on about the fifteenth one. He must be seven hundred years old by now.'

Cass cleared her throat, and immediately got our attention. 'Do you know what time you were born, Finn?'

'Err, let me think. Nope, don't remember. Maybe I was busy – screaming or crapping myself, or whatever babies do,' I said sarcastically. I thought she'd find it funny, but she didn't.

Cass pulled some paper from the file, an official-looking certificate.

'I do,' she said, and for some reason I felt an ache in the side of my chest. Like the blunt tip of a wooden stake was pressing into my ribs. The sun was nearer the ridge of the valley now. Daylight was retreating, and the flames of the fire seemed brighter. Cass handed me the certificate, then added another log to the fire.

'You were born at thirteen minutes past one, on the afternoon of June thirteenth.'

Squid looked momentarily confused, but for once I was ahead of him.

'Is that five thirteen in the morning, California time?'

'Exactly.' Cass nodded slowly.

She turned on the lamp next to me. The ink on the certificate was faint, but I could have read it anyway; the room wasn't that dark, not yet. And in the warm lamplight, the printed words were unmistakeable.

'*Finnegan Malcolm Quick …*' I read slowly. '*Date of birth: Friday, thirteenth June. Time of birth: thirteen thirteen.*'

'Jeez, that's a lot of unlucky,' said Squid; he was on his feet beside me.

'What d'you mean?' said Cass.

'Well, all of it. Everything. Friday the thirteenth, all those thirteens, *Malcolm.*'

He had a point. I've always hated my middle name.

'So you're here because of me? Your dad moved all the way here to England because I was born the exact minute your mum died?'

132

Cass laughed. 'There's a bit more to it than that. Have another look at the birth certificate.'

'How did your dad get this again?' I asked, squinting at it. But that's when I saw what she meant. The sections for *Mother* and *Father* were empty. Just blank.

'I've got no parents,' I said, looking up, tears unexpectedly filling my eyes. Squid grabbed the certificate to look for himself.

'That's how Dad realised it must be you. No one has no parents.'

'But that's not possible,' said Squid. 'Even Jesus had one parent.'

'My dad got the birth certificates for every kid on the planet born at the same time as you.'

'But there must be thousands,' said Squid, still studying the certificate.

'No, there are two hundred and seventy-one, they're all in this file,' she said, holding it higher. 'And of all the two hundred and seventy-one, you're the only one without parents.'

'I did have a mum and dad.' I could feel tears spill as I said it. 'I can still remember them. I can draw them if you like – every tiny detail.' I looked at Squid, then back at Cass. Even she looked worried. Like I might have a meltdown or something.

'I don't care what this bit of paper says – *I did have a mum and dad*.'

There are no photos of them, but I've sketched Mum and Dad a million times. And I always carry a picture of them. Always. I dug it out of my pocket and unfolded the paper. It was my best sketch and it was pretty good. Mum and Dad smiling, Biscuit sitting at their feet, all in front of the house, like they were posing for a photograph.

'Is that them?' asked Squid, and all I could do was nod. And try not to cry.

'Look, I get it,' said Cass. 'And so does Dad. That's why we came here – to investigate.' She looked at Squid, and spoke plainly. 'Finn dreamed them away – his mum and dad. That's why they disappeared.'

Squid's face froze into a mask of disgust and pity, and I had to look away.

We sat there in silence for a long while. Me staring out of the window, my mind a blank. Beyond the church, the sun was falling. And from this angle it looked like it was going to be spiked on the spire. I watched, lost with my thoughts, as the dropping sun gently kissed the cross at the top of the steeple.

'But why *move* here?' asked Squid. 'Why buy a house and move everything here? All this –' he waved at the stacked files covering the table and filling the chairs. 'No one just moves their entire life to the other side of the world f—'

'Stop talking.' Cass held up her hand as if she were telling a dog to sit. Squid stopped talking and sat back down. 'Just let me finish. The important bit, the bit you need to know, is that after my mum died … well, she kept coming back.'

'What? How?'

'Dad's never really understood it. But trust me, he's not making it up. Somehow, she was able to come back, in dreams. Not all the time, not even very often. But every now and again, she comes back.'

'But that's normal,' objected Squid. 'We dream about people all the time – dead or alive. It's not weird at all.'

Cass smiled. 'You don't understand. Yeah, sure, we dream about people – like we might dream about things. But also, we dream *with* people.'

'What do you mean?' I asked.

'Like last night – you weren't dreaming about us two. You were dreaming *with* us. Do you see the difference?'

I looked at Squid and he gave me a shrug.

Cass took another sip from her bottle. 'Dad says he dreamed about her right away. After she died, I mean.

135

That first night she was there in his bedroom, shouting, screaming at him. Demanding that he help bring her back. He says she was often pretty angry even when she was alive, but after the car accident, it was like she was a different person. Like her soul had been … corrupted.'

'Corrupted?' said Squid. Cass looked at him; her face was tight.

'Yeah, corrupted. That's the word he used. The trouble with having everything, he used to say, is that when you die, you *lose* everything. And maybe when she died, that was all too much.'

'But what has any of this got to do with us?' I couldn't help asking. 'You still haven't even answered our first question. What are you really doing here?'

Cass stood, obviously unhappy. She walked to the big windows and looked out on to the garden. The sun had half disappeared over the ridge of the valley, but you could still see out, just. See the garden, and the church beyond, its spire now silhouetted black against the greying sky. Images of the graveyard and the crypt popped into my head uninvited, and I immediately pushed them away.

'A few months ago,' said Cass, with her back to us, 'Dad dreamed about her again. He says she seemed worse than ever – angry, desperate.'

'Desperate for what?' asked Squid.

'For information. But this time, about just one thing.'
Cass turned to face me, and I knew what she was going
to say. 'Mum was only interested in you, Finnegan
Malcolm Quick.'

'So that's why you're here?' I could hear that my voice
was too loud, but I couldn't seem to control it. 'You and
your dad have come all the way to England to snoop
around for her.'

'Don't be stupid. We're not here to help her.' Cass bit
her lip before finishing. 'We came here to stop her
killing you.'

My tongue went stiff in my mouth. I couldn't speak.
All I could do was sit there and look at Cass's serious
face. She looked angry.

The outside was almost black now and the room felt
different. The light from the little lamp was feeble, and
the big old library felt smaller, like it was being erased
by shadows.

'Can we get some more lights on?' I said, regaining
my voice.

'Sure,' said Cass. 'It's a lot to take in.'

Squid helped, turning on the half-dozen lamps
dotted around the room while I just sat there. He was
obviously feeling creeped out too, because he moved
fast. And Squid never moves fast.

When, eventually, we settled back down in the chairs by the fire, Cass pulled out an old leather notebook.

'You asked me before why I screamed when I saw the woman in the crypt. Well, it's because I recognised her. From this sketch in my dad's dream diary.' She handed me the journal and I looked with a rising sense of dread. 'Dad drew it, from one of his dreams. It's my mum,' she finished quietly.

'That's her,' I said. 'The woman from my dreams, from the crypt.'

The sketch was in pencil, but every last detail was there: the slashes across her face and the scar running down her throat; the ragged bandages soaked with blood.

'Is that really your mum?' I said, unable to take my eyes off the image.

Cass shifted awkwardly. 'Yes ... and no. It's *what she's become.*'

Squid was leaning over my shoulder, his face horrified. 'Oh wow, she's a total monster.'

Cass flinched when he said that. Actually physically flinched. She quickly closed the notebook, flicking around the elastic bands to keep it shut tight.

'Sorry,' said Squid, embarrassed.

'It's OK,' said Cass, but it clearly wasn't. She sat back

down. 'It's not really my mum. It's just what's left of her … distorted soul.'

We sat in awkward silence, no one really knowing what to say. Eventually Cass spoke again.

'Dad says she was totally different in life. I obviously don't remember, but Dad says when he first met her, she was like the brightest, funniest, most brilliant person you ever met.'

'So what happened?' Squid couldn't take his eyes off the notebook in Cass's hand, even though it was firmly closed.

Cass stood again, and started pacing. As if she wanted to walk away from difficult thoughts. It was obviously hard to talk about her mum like this, but she seemed determined.

'I don't really know. Dad's got lots of theories. Lack of sleep probably didn't help – she limited herself to four hours a day, so she could control things better.'

'Control things?' I asked.

'Yeah. It's easier to control dreams if you keep them short. And by the end she was sleeping in little twenty-minute bursts.'

'That's enough to unhinge anybody,' said Squid. Then he looked at me, suddenly awkward. Both of us were painfully aware of how little sleep I'd had over the last week. Was I becoming unhinged too?

'But it was more than that,' Cass continued. 'Dad says it had something to do with her parents. She never spoke about them, about how they died, and it was like some hideous dark secret that ate away at her. By the time of the car crash Dad says she was getting more and more angry. And then, well, I guess to have all that power one minute, and then lose it all … I guess it just pushed her over the edge.'

I looked at Squid and he shifted in his chair. Clearly it was up to me to say something.

'Look,' I said finally. 'I think it's time we met your dad.'

Cass laughed at that, and nodded. 'Of course. You've waited ages.' She instinctively turned to the windows and the now dark evening sky. 'The door's unlocked, just go on through.'

She invited us towards the study and, like two little obedient puppies, we sprang up. Squid moved ahead to open the door, but hesitated with his hand on the brass handle. Probably imagining what Cass's dad would actually be like, in the flesh.

The handle unlatched and he pushed gently, the door swinging easily into a darkened room.

'The lights are off,' said Squid, unease creeping into his voice.

'Yeah, about that. There's one other thing I need to tell you,' said Cass, reaching past Squid to flick on the light switch. 'I know this is going to sound weird, but my dad … He's not completely alive either.'

Most people would expect to run in a situation like that. And I must admit, it did cross my mind.

But Squid was already half trapped in the room, and besides, where would I run to? The house was a total maze. I'd get lost. Then I'd hide, and then I'd be hunted down in some deadly game of hide-and-seek. It's bad enough when that happens in dreams, but in real life? No thank you.

So instead, I did what I often do when faced with bowel-erupting danger. I froze.

The light came on and Squid immediately started backing away. 'Mate, you're not gonna believe this,' he said, treading on my foot. 'There's a coffin.'

I looked at Cass in horror.

'Your dad's a vampire?' I whispered harshly.

'What?' She laughed. She laughed right in my face, so close I could smell her breath. She'd been eating cucumber.

Something didn't add up.

'Of course he's not a vampire, you idiot. He's in some sort of sleep paralysis.'

· 'What's he doing in a bloody coffin then?' Squid blurted out. Then he started inching back into the study to get another look. Sometimes Squid has got more guts than I give him credit for.

Cass looked annoyed. 'Look, that was the only way to get him into the country, all right? The paperwork's a nightmare.'

'But why's he still in there?'

Cass looked at Squid as if he were stupid. 'He weighs two hundred pounds, why'd you think?'

I could see the coffin myself now, resting on a long table. Two slippered feet stuck up at the far end. And from this angle, I could make out neatly combed black hair on the top of his head.

As you can imagine, we crept our way inside that study slowly. But when we finally got a proper look, Cass's dad was surprisingly ordinary. Just your average, run-of-the-mill, middle-aged man. You know, big forehead, bigger nose. It's weird, you don't often look at middle-aged men when they're asleep. Well, I don't. He looked tired even though he was asleep, and that doesn't even seem possible.

'He looks like a waxwork,' said Squid.

The skin did look thick and waxy, like it might not be real, and I was suddenly tempted to give his face a poke, just in case this was some weird practical joke.

And I couldn't help feeling, as we stood looking at him, that I'd seen him somewhere before.

'Why the grandad slippers?' asked Squid, looking at the tartan check as though it might be some important clue.

'Look, just come back out, will you.' Cass gave the sleeve of Squid's hoody a yank, and soon we were back in the library, the study door firmly shut behind us.

'I don't mean to be funny,' said Squid, 'but why is he in slippers if he's in a coma?'

Cass gave him another one of her looks. 'He's not in a coma, it's a sleep paralysis. And the slippers are just to cover his feet up. Have you ever looked at an adult's feet? Trust me, they're better covered up.'

'Does anyone come in to look after him?' I said, trying to get the conversation back on track. 'I mean, a nurse or someone?'

'He's fine. It's all OK.' Cass's face reddened and she slumped on to the arm of the leather sofa. 'Look, if the doctors see him, it's game over. It's one of Dad's rules – never force someone awake who's trapped in a dream. God knows what they'd do to him in a hospital.' She took a swig from her bottle of juice and swallowed it loudly.

'What happens if you break the rule?' asked Squid.

'Bad happens. Real bad.' Cass was starting to look annoyed again. 'Look, he's done this before, as part of his research. Just … not for this long.'

'How long has he been like this?' I asked.

'Since May.'

'Since *May*?'

I felt bad as soon as I'd blurted it out. Cass immediately stood. Her eyes were red, like she was about to cry.

'He's fine, OK? He's got a pulse, but it's slow. Really slow. And he hardly breathes. He's in some sort of stasis. He's fine.'

'So what happened in May?' asked Squid.

'I don't know.' Cass shook her head, suddenly looking tired. 'It was just after we bought this place, but before we actually moved here. Dad had two dreams about Mum, close together – but he didn't give me the full details. He told me about you, and that he was worried Mum was going to do something. Something bad. Then he had about a week when he hardly slept, and he was getting more and more stressed. And then, one night … one night he went to sleep and … never woke up.'

We carried on with more questions. But to be honest, we didn't really learn much more. After her dad had gone into his coma-sleep thing, Cass had panicked. And then she'd gone through all his papers, and his dream diary, and gradually started piecing things together. God knows how she'd managed to get to England. Flying international when you're a kid is hard enough – but doing it with a 'dead' body?

All she'd say on that was, 'You'd be amazed what you can do with money.'

It was getting late by the time we ran out of questions, and the fire was almost gone.

'There's one thing you haven't asked about,' she said, gathering up her dad's leather notebook from where she'd left it on the table. 'You still haven't asked me about the crypt. And why we went there.'

I felt pretty stupid about that. I had never asked – about any of it. Maybe I just wanted to forget that afternoon had ever happened. Maybe I was just afraid she wanted us to go back and try again.

'Go on then,' I said eventually.

'Well, I don't completely understand it. But there are more sketches in Dad's notebook,' she said, peeling off the elastic bands. 'He drew all sorts of stuff. See what you make of it.'

She handed me the open notebook, and Squid immediately leaped up to get a better look.

'That's the old church crypt,' he said, recognising it instantly.

'I know. Turn the page,' she said.

I turned the page to find another drawing, this time of the inside of the mausoleum; that first room with the steps leading down.

'Turn again,' said Cass.

The third image was of the sarcophagus, the one we'd spectacularly failed to open. Her dad had even drawn the rows of coffins – tucked away in their vaults within the far wall. At the bottom of the page, in neat, old-fashioned handwriting, were written three words:

Find his parents.

'You're doing all this because of those three words?' I said. 'Do you even know why your dad wrote that?'

'Nope.' Cass let out a laugh. 'But it's all there is. The only clue we've got.'

'Why would your dad care so much?' I said. 'I mean, why come here – all the way from California – to this …?' I looked around at the room. 'This creepy old Freak House with a library with no books, and bedrooms with bars and nightmares on the walls. Why?'

'You know, ever since I found Dad's notebook, I've been asking myself that exact question. But he did care.

Dad wanted to help you. He wanted to find your mum and dad.'

'And that's how he ended up in a coffin wearing old grandad slippers,' added Squid.

I would have laughed, but as he said it, and I watched the irritation flare across Cass's face, something became clear in my mind.

'Oh God, that's why you brought us here tonight,' I said, the realisation punching me in the stomach. 'You want to go back to the crypt.'

'Back to the crypt?' echoed Squid. 'Where you almost died?'

'But we didn't die. We *learned*,' she said.

I couldn't quite believe what I was hearing. 'Learned? What exactly did we learn? How to be ripped apart by zombies?'

'Don't be so dramatic, we learned loads.' She took back the leather notepad and flicked to the back page, and a list in her own handwriting. 'We learned three key things. One, we need weapons, for neutralising zombies and … anything else that tries to stop us.'

We all knew what she really meant by 'anything else': her mum.

'Like what sort of weapon?'

'Like that sort of weapon.' Cass pointed to the

mantelpiece above the fire. I hadn't noticed before, but there were four small water pistols sitting there.

'Water pistols?' said Squid, clearly as unimpressed as I was.

'No, *holy* water pistols. They're filled with holy water, from the church. You saw what happened to the goblin, right?'

'But that was a goblin, a demon,' said Squid. 'These are zombies – your mum's a zombie too, right?'

Squid paused to give Cass a chance to answer, but she didn't.

'Well,' continued Squid. 'Zombies, demons, totally different. You need totally different weapons.' He looked at the water pistols, neatly propped on the mantelpiece. 'This would be like taking garlic to a werewolf fight. It's never gonna work, not in a million years.'

'You still don't get it, do you?' answered Cass. 'Do you know why that goblin exploded when we hit it with holy water?'

'Not exactly. Is it not just … what demons do?' answered Squid.

'No, the reason that goblin exploded – *the only reason* – is because we believed it would. So get with the plan. Believe in them, and these holy water pistols will totally work.'

Cass handed me two of the pistols, keeping two for herself.

'What about me?' said Squid, suddenly showing a bit more faith in holy water.

'You're staying here. That's the second thing we learned. We need proper insurance. If something goes wrong, it's your job to wake us.'

'But what if I can't? Last time it was almost impossible. I virtually had to punch you.'

'Then punch us again. And if that doesn't work, punch harder.'

'And if it still doesn't work?' asked Squid.

'There are hot coals there,' she said, pointing to the fire. 'Use them if you have to.'

'What's the third thing?' I asked, swallowing hard.

'The third thing is Betty,' said Cass, with a rare smile. She reached under the sofa and with difficulty dragged out what seemed to be some sort of giant hammer. 'This is to smash through the lid of the sarcophagus.'

'That's a sledgehammer,' said Squid.

'I call her Betty.'

'Can you even lift Betty?'

'I can in a dream.'

'Hold on,' I objected. 'I don't get this. Why do we need any of this in real life? Why don't we just dream it up?'

Cass looked at me as though I were simple.

'These are physical props. Remember when you were a little kid and you played, I dunno, with action figures or dolls or whatever? The toys helped you make-believe. This is the same. Because down there in the crypt, it won't be enough to believe, we need to *really* believe.'

'But why?' I asked, struggling to understand.

'You remember last time? What happened to the torches?'

I nodded. 'They went out? Is that because—?'

'Someone believed more strongly than we did,' said Cass, finishing my sentence.

'Hold on, you're honestly telling me someone believed your batteries flat?' said Squid. 'Who?'

Cass shrugged. 'Probably my mum. She was special, remember. Powerful. That's why you need to focus, Finn. *Really* focus.'

'But why me?'

'Because you're special too,' she said, her face softening.

Squid couldn't help laughing at the word 'special'. Cass ignored him.

'My dad thought so. He told me about you, before … you know.' She looked towards the study, and I thought of her father, lying there peacefully in his coffin. 'He said he'd seen you. That's why he called you a superhero of dreams — because he saw what you were capable of.'

'A *superhero*? You've got to be kidding!' Squid said out loud what I was thinking.

'Yeah, you can imagine how disappointed I've been,' said Cass, and unexpectedly my heart went tight in my chest.

'Dad said you could do properly impressive stuff. But only when you weren't running away. Do you even remember seeing him?'

'Kind of, he looks familiar, but …' I shook my head. 'Did he say when? Or where?'

'According to his dream diary, he was coming to this place a lot — to the cemetery, and the crypt, I mean. I assume it was then. You really can't remember?'

'No. I have so many dreams — besides I've spent most of my life trying to forget them.' I suddenly felt hot, even though the fire had burned itself low. 'What did he say I could do, exactly?'

'He said you had more belief, more conviction and more faith than anyone he'd ever met. Even Mum. Maybe that's why your dreams cross back into reality.'

I didn't know what to say to that. It didn't seem likely. I've never been special at anything. Unless you count being afraid.

Squid and I looked at each other. Eventually I said, 'You're forgetting. There's a fourth thing we learned about the crypt.'

'What's that?' said Cass.

'That we should never, ever go anywhere near it, ever again.'

'You still don't get it, do you?' Cass was struggling to hold Betty, and let it drop to the floor. 'If we don't do this, if we don't find your parents – then she'll be back, for your gran. And she won't just send one goblin, she'll send dozens, or a troll, or whatever she can dream up. And after your gran's gone, she'll come for you. Doing this, finding your mum and dad, it's the only way.'

I knew she was right, even before she said it. But I knew something else too.

'But that's not why you're doing this, is it?'

'What do you mean?' she said, frowning hard.

'Those sketches in your dad's notebook. You think that's where he went – the last time he slept. You think he's down there too, in the crypt.'

'Yeah, so?'

'So you're not doing this to save me, or my gran, or Mum and Dad. You're doing this because you think if you save my parents, you might be able to save your own dad.'

The frown left her face, and Cass suddenly looked weary, almost old. For a second I thought her face was going to crumple into a sob. But it didn't.

'Sure, why not,' she said eventually. 'Let's just say our goals are aligned. Perfectly.'

15

RETURN TO THE CRYPT

There was no arguing after that. With all cards on the table, there was only one possible conclusion. Whether it was to find my parents, save Gran or rescue Cass's dad, there was no other choice. We had to go back to the crypt.

After more discussion, we decided to set up base camp in the library. It might not be exactly cosy, but it was a damn sight less bleak than the rest of the house. Squid and I built up the fire with fresh wood, while Cass went to get mattresses.

It gave me and Squid a few precious moments alone.

'You know this is insane, right?' Squid was close to the fire and he looked sweaty. 'Those zombie things would have killed you last time. And Cass's mum? She's a complete monster.'

'Pretty much,' I said, pulling a face. 'But what choice do I have? We have to do something. Cass was right. That woman has been after me all my life. And she'll keep coming back – not just for me, but for Gran too. I know she will.'

I'd told Squid all about our first crypt dream, but he insisted on going through it again, step by step.

'You need to move faster,' he said. 'The last time you wasted too much time. Get in, get the sarcophagus-thingy open, get your mum and dad, and get out.'

'What if I can't get them out?' I said.

'Then we'll do this again,' interrupted Cass from the doorway. She was struggling with the mattresses. 'And again, for as long as it takes. Each time we go back, we learn something new.'

'But so do the zombies.' I jumped up to help. 'You said it yourself. They learn too, they get smarter.'

'Which is why we need to get smarter, *quicker*.'

We carried the mattresses over to the fireplace, pulled back the sofa and chairs to make space, and then arranged everything in a fan around the open fire. It took a while to get ready, but eventually we all settled down on to our makeshift beds.

'Squid, what are you doing?' I said. He'd found a sandwich in his overnight bag and had started eating it.

'Peanut butter,' he said, offering me some. 'Helps me relax before bed.'

'You're unbelievable. You're not supposed to relax – you're supposed to stay alert, awake.'

'Sorry, I forgot,' he said, but took another bite anyway.

Cass gave me a look that for once was more smile than frown. 'Squid, your job – your *only* job – is to stay awake. Please tell me you've got this.'

'I've got this,' he said, finishing the sandwich. 'And the first sign that anything's wrong, I'm going to wake you. This time we're taking no chances.'

Cass nodded, and turned to me.

'Now, Finn, are you ready? It's beddy-bye time.'

Again, Cass fell asleep more or less straight away. How she does it so quick I have no idea. But I just lay there, reliving past dreams. Thinking of those zombies, and the woman at the gates – could it really be Cass's mum? Could I really trust Cass, when it came down to it? The power of her mum's hands, as she squeezed the bars like they were cooked noodles, was horrifying. In my mind's eye, I could see her clearly – a mixture of the creature I'd dreamed and the one Cass's dad had drawn.

A 'complete monster', Squid had called her. All because she'd been cursed with the same power I'd been cursed with.

And then my mind flicked away – to the goblin, and how it had felt when the creature touched my foot. This time, I was keeping my shoes on.

That was something else I'd learned. Maybe Cass was right, I remember thinking; maybe, with all the knowledge we had now, maybe there was a way out of this mess. Maybe, just maybe, I was only one sleep away from seeing Mum and Dad.

'*Finn,*' whispered Squid. 'Are you awake? I've been thinking. You don't kill a zombie with holy water. You just don't. You have to blow them up, or chop their heads off. Everyone knows that. Fire works too – they're terrified of it.'

'Shut up, Squid. I just have to believe in the water pistols, remember?'

'I told you – you're taking garlic to a werewolf fight. Why not take a log too? Just in case, eh?' He took one of the logs we'd stacked up by the fireplace and tried to hand it to me. It was long and heavy, and for a moment I was tempted. 'Keep one water pistol, but carry this too. You can even take some matches to light it.'

'No, Squid, it's too heavy. And anyway, it'll only blow out just when I need it.'

157

'But—'

'But nothing. You're not helping. I need to believe in the water pistols.'

I had a water pistol in each hand, and I squeezed them tight. It's an old sleep hack Gran taught me: tense your muscles as hard as you can, then let them relax. Keep doing it and, sooner or later, you'll fall asleep.

This night was no exception. And squeezing for dear life, I drifted off into a troubled sleep.

I sat up to find Squid staring into the fire, picking his nose thoughtfully. Cass was already standing, leaning on Betty, the sledgehammer. She gave me a look and a jerk of her head, as if to say, 'Come on, let's get out of here before he eats it.'

The windowed doors on to the garden opened easily, but I hesitated. There's something about going from light to dark that always makes me wary. Cass seemed to understand; there was an outside light for the terrace, a little hanging lantern, and she turned it on.

'Put your pistols in your pockets and get your torch ready,' she said quietly. 'We want to be quick, OK? In and out.'

We ran across the lawn, and easily found the opening in the brick wall. The old wooden door was already unlocked, and with practised ease, Cass dragged it open.

Getting to the crypt was easy too, but our first obstacle was immediately obvious. Even by the light of the torches it was clear that the bars of the metal gates were still wrapped tightly on to each other. I thought back to the first crypt dream with a shudder.

'I'd totally forgotten,' I whispered, painfully aware that we needed to be quiet.

'I hadn't,' said Cass, and she pulled out a small hacksaw from her rucksack. 'Hold the torch there. This won't take long – I've sawn most of the way through already.'

I held the torch while she worked, and marvelled at the speed with which she broke through it. The twisted bars must have been hanging by a thread of iron because with a few thrusts of the saw, the bar fell – clanging on to the stone floor, horrifically loud.

'We're in,' she said, and the gates swung silently apart.

I've done some terrifying things in dreams. I've hidden in wardrobes while faceless men searched my room, I've run from gargoyles across frozen lakes, and I've even been buried alive, holding my breath as were-wolves tried to dig me up. But I'm telling you, for pure, undiluted terror, nothing took more guts than walking through those metal gates and into the crypt.

We didn't waste time, just went straight down the stairs and into the lower chamber. Cass immediately positioned herself by the sarcophagus.

'Stand back, I don't want to bash your brains out,' she said, lifting Betty level with her waist.

I took a step back, exploring the walls with my torch. Light danced from coffin to coffin, each exactly as we'd first seen them – safely enclosed in their tight little vaults.

The thump as Betty smashed into the lid of the sarcophagus was enormous. It echoed so loudly my ears were still ringing when Cass struck a second time. And then even she had to jump back. Splinters of stone exploded everywhere, and as the slab broke apart, it slid crashing to the floor.

I ran forward, ignoring the dust, to help Cass push away the remaining stone. And I looked into the sarcophagus with a trembling torch.

What we found, without word of a lie, is possibly the strangest thing I've ever seen.

At first, it seemed like a pool of swirling light. I thought the sarcophagus must be filled with some sort of glowing water. But there was something immediately and obviously wrong with that theory, because despite being bright as a bulb, nothing shone into the room. Like a light bulb sucking *in* light, not beaming it out. Does that make sense? Probably not.

'Well, I wasn't expecting that,' said Cass, with massive understatement.

I did what most people would do in a situation like that and, unthinking, reached out to touch it with my hand.

Warmth flowed into my fingertips, and then up my arm until it consumed my entire body. It filled me with happiness. No, more than that – I felt *swollen* with it. A sense that everything would be OK. I shut my eyes and gave in to the sensations: arms around me, holding me, lifting me – like I was just a little baby. And when I opened my eyes, there was Mum, smiling at me. I could even smell her. A smell I'd all but forgotten of cotton and lemons and sunshine. If I could just push on deeper into the light, I knew I could stay here, next to my mum, forever.

'What are you doing?' Cass yanked my arm away, and suddenly I was blinking fast as my head spun back to reality. To the damp, gloomy chamber, surrounded by death and decay.

My first urge was to scream at her. I think I did shout, with the anger and sadness of having it all snatched away, my brain swaying like I'd just stepped off a boat or a roller coaster.

'It's a gateway,' said Cass, calmly but firmly. 'Don't touch it. Dad says they're dangerous.'

'Gateway to where?'

'Really? You wanna do questions? Now?' She looked up at the coffins filling the far wall as if to make the point, but I ignored her.

'Yes, I do want to do questions now. Tell me. Gateway to where?'

Cass lowered her voice but never once took her eyes off the far wall.

'Have you never read about near-death experiences?'

'What, where people almost die and they see a tunnel of light to …?' I trailed off and Cass finished my sentence.

'To the next life. And that, Finnegan Quick, is a tunnel of light.'

I looked back down at the churning pool. A pattern was forming in the random swirls of light.

'So what do we do now?' I said, unable to take my eyes off it.

Cass put a hand on my shoulder, and I slowly felt myself being pulled back from the sarcophagus.

'Finn, I need you to focus. I was wrong about the sarcophagus. But I'm sure my dad's here somewhere.

You're not going to like this – but we're going to have to open up some of those coffins.'

Immediately my eyes snapped away from the light.

'You have to be kidding me!' I tried to say more, but my mouth just moved uselessly.

Cass's voice was calm and slow. 'No, we have to do this. Dad has to be here somewhere. Your parents might be in there too.'

'*Might* be?' I repeated disbelievingly.

'Yes, they might.' Cass's stare was emphatic. 'There's no point coming down here if we're just going to run away at the first setback,' she finished.

I thought of Gran. *You've got to face your fears sometime, boy, or they'll bite you on the bum*, she always says. But I've never really believed it. If you run fast enough, *nothing* can get you – that's what I believe. After all these years of nightmares, I was living proof of it.

But this was different. This time, running away wouldn't help.

I looked over at the rows of coffins, all end on, tidily tucked away in their tight little cubbyholes. Each holding a body. I thought of the rotten corpses that had come crashing out before. And wondered why they hadn't come again.

Move faster, Squid had said, but we'd already been

down here for ages. And we hadn't exactly been quiet. I looked at the coffins, half expecting one to come sliding out, just like before.

'Where do we even start?' I said, still not really believing we'd go through with it.

'Newest coffins first,' said Cass, breathing a nervous sigh away. 'Remember, you've got the water pistols, and in a dream you're powerful. You're a superhero – in your dreams.'

She said the last words with a smile, but I wasn't sure whether it was kind or sarcastic. And with a pistol gripped firm in my left hand, and my torch in the other, I followed her over to the wall of coffins.

'Try that one,' she said, tapping her torch on to the shiny brass handle of a pristine-looking coffin. The pale wood was polished, like it had been put there only yesterday. I reached forward and pulled.

The coffin slid out surprisingly easily. The runners had obviously been well greased because the whole casket came out with barely any force. In the white torchlight, the varnished wood shone.

'Open it,' she whispered. 'The lid should just slide off.' Her torch was still in one hand, but I now saw she had a water pistol in the other – pointed firmly at the head of the coffin.

I've never opened a coffin before. I bet you haven't either. I doubt many people have. It's not like grave-robbing is big business any more. I kind of assumed it would be nailed on or something, but Cass was right, the lid just slid sideways. Polished wood slid over polished wood as a pulse drummed a steady beat in my neck. And then the rhythm went berserk as Cass's torch shone into the open coffin.

'It's the Maere!' she whispered harshly and need-lessly. The goblin was lying on its back, head pillowed on raised arms, like it was sunbathing or maybe cloud watching on a summer's afternoon. There was even a closed plastic umbrella resting across its lap.

As if that wasn't weird enough, it still wore the helmet – well, what was left of it. Because the goblin had been preserved exactly as I'd last seen it: its head sliced half away. I made the mistake of glancing inside the empty walnut shell of its helmet-encased skull, and immediately regretted it.

'But we destroyed it?' I said, annoyed to hear the whine in my voice.

Cass shrugged. 'I guess the Heinrich treatment wasn't permanent. Come on, try another.'

The coffin next along was older than the first, but still new. Cass's dad had been gone for months and the level of dirt and dust looked about right. I pointed, Cass nodded, and we pulled the second coffin out of its vault.

This time the lid was harder to shift, as if glued with grime. But with both of us working, it eventually came off too. And there, inside the second coffin, in precisely the position he occupied in real life … was Cass's dad.

Now I saw him again, I did recognise him. I see a lot of people in dreams so it's no surprise I forget some. But this man had been there more than once. Mostly as a *lurker*, someone skulking in the background, watching but never really doing anything. But as I looked down at him in the coffin, his peaceful expression suggesting a dreamless sleep, one particular dream popped out of my memory: a dream of a cemetery, with him showing me round, pointing out old gravestones, with smiles and a kind face.

I looked up at Cass. She had tears in her eyes, and I instinctively wanted to look away. But with her jaw clenched, she looked right at me – unembarrassed. Her voice, when it came out, was tight.

'We need to get him out,' she said. And pulling him up towards her chest, she started lifting him from the open coffin. The strength it took must have been immense. At first I wondered why she even tried, but soon remembered: in dreams, Cass has unbelievable strength.

Dropping her torch, she managed to heave him out. He was tall, and she had to drag him across the floor.

'Come on, I can't do the stairs on my own.'

I stood there, staring. 'What about me? What about my parents?'

'We'll come back. I promise. Dad will help. But we need to save him first.'

My mind twisted through a dozen thoughts. *That's not fair*, was the first one, but they got uglier. From anger to desperation, my brain didn't know where to turn. And in the end, it never got to decide. Because right then, while Cass and I stood staring at each other, the goblin sat up in its coffin. A happy grin showed sharp, hungry teeth, as if we'd just given it a box of chocolates.

'Shoot it!' shouted Cass, but I was already ahead of her. I had a water pistol in my left hand and I squirted. But if I was one move ahead of Cass, the goblin was ahead of both of us. The umbrella came up fast and the water bounced away, drumming off the plastic. It was see-through, a little kid's umbrella, and as I fired again, the goblin's smile didn't even flicker.

Then it started climbing to the floor and I fired again, lower, at its legs – but the creature's reactions were lightning fast. I kept firing but the umbrella always seemed to be there, like a Jedi lightsaber deflecting a blaster.

Cass was disappearing up the steps, dragging her dad. 'Just hold it off, I'll come back when I've got Dad safe,' she said.

I retreated steadily, buying as much time as I could, always walking backwards up the steps, terrified I'd slip. And then out, and into the cemetery – firing whenever I needed to slow it down. One pistol went dry and I threw it at the goblin. But the gun just bounced off the umbrella like everything else.

Cass was long gone; desperation gives you strength, I guess. My last remaining pistol no longer felt heavy, it was near empty, and the goblin seemed bolder than ever, dancing between the gravestones.

'Come on!' screamed Cass from behind me. She was at the door in the wall. 'Dad's safe, back at the house. Just run!'

I fired the pistol, determined to do just that – but only a dribble came out. The goblin's smile grew huge. He was now close enough that if I tried to run, he'd *get me*.

I thought of the lump of firewood Squid had offered me. I'd have given anything for that right now. The goblin lowered its umbrella. It was so close, I could almost smell it. And then I watched transfixed as its hand reached towards me, watched those fingers as they seemed to grow, stretching towards me.

The pulse in my neck and ears was a thrum of noise, and I'm ashamed to say I just shut my eyes, and waited for the end.

'Just think of something, you idiot,' said Cass from behind me. But all I could think about was Squid's lump of wood. And what an idiot I'd been to turn it down.

Now, that moment could easily have been my last. Another touch from that goblin, and I'm pretty sure my heart wouldn't have survived it. But the power of dreams is an incredible thing. It's something I'm still only really beginning to understand. Because standing there, ready to die, I felt something suddenly growing in my hand, getting heavy. And I opened my eyes to see Squid's lump of wood. It was even lit – burning fiercely at one end. The goblin looked confused. Not worried, just confused. And then something else: disgust, like I was holding a giant poo. And with a sudden elation at my power, I chucked the burning log. Right in its face.

I didn't wait to see what happened next.

I turned to Cass, and I ran.

Cass reached the house with unbelievable speed. I ran fast too, and never looked back, not once. But I could hear the goblin behind me – snuffling as it ran on all fours across the lawn. I sprinted into the house, slamming the glass doors shut behind me, pushing until I heard the clunk of the latch. The goblin must have been only metres behind, because it arrived a second later, smacking into the glass.

Unbelievably, the door didn't break. Maybe I somehow dreamed it strong, I don't know. All I know is that the helmeted goblin slammed into that door and, like a cartoon figure, slid to the ground, its face squashed against the glass. There was a lock and I flipped it shut, painfully aware how fragile the glass windows were against a sustained attack.

'Cass,' I shouted, turning to her. 'This won't hold for long; we need to get—'

I never finished the sentence because I immediately saw something was wrong. The lamps were off, only firelight remained, and the feeble light from the terrace lantern. And in that light, I saw Cass standing, staring.

'Where's your dad?'

'He's gone,' she said, eyes massive in the gloom.

'I'm sorry,' said a voice from one of the armchairs, and I looked across to see Squid, lit by firelight. He looked tiny, as if the chair had suddenly grown, or maybe he'd shrunk. He was tiny and pink, sweating from the heat of the fire.

'Squid, what are you doing here? You're not supposed to be in the dream,' I said, as the goblin thumped into the glass a second time. This time I heard a crack as one of the panes began to splinter.

'I'm sorry,' said Squid again. And I immediately understood.

'Squid, you idiot, you just had one job.'

Squid was our insurance policy. Our guarantee that we'd wake, that we'd escape from this nightmare with our lives intact. And he'd fallen asleep.

'I told you not to eat that peanut butter sandwich.'

'She took him away,' said Squid, and I immediately knew who. But I had to ask. I had to be sure.

'Who took him, Squid?'

He looked at me blankly, his whole body rigid.

'The woman. The woman did. The woman with no eyes.'

I looked to Cass, expecting her to shout, but she just stood there, motionless, silent, listening. And even before we heard, it was clear there was someone, or something, else with us in the house.

'You've done well.' The voice came from the shadows of the hallway beyond the library door. It came as a long

171

rasp, like a metal saw slowly being drawn across glass – but quiet, as if muffled or far away. 'It's time to stop now. It's time to give up,' said the voice.

I looked at Cass and her eyes warned me to stay quiet. But for some idiot reason, I spoke.

'Look, I don't know what you want. If you think I've taken your power – I haven't. Well, if I have, I don't want it. Just take it back. Just take everything.'

'Yes, *everything*,' repeated the voice. 'Only then will you be ready.'

She laughed, and it echoed into the room unexpectedly loud – gurgling, as if the woman's throat was still full of blood. She laughed, and the fire guttered. As if that laugh was sucking the oxygen out of the room, choking the fire to death. And then the laughing stopped, leaving just an echo, as the fire sputtered out, to black.

The outside light from the terrace lantern was all there was now. It made shadows on the wall, a grid of squares where the light shone through the small panes of glass. And there we all were, like characters in a shadow play: Squid's silhouette, tiny in his giant chair; and Cass standing, utterly motionless. My shadow was there too, and I stood looking at it, listening, waiting for the next move. I didn't have to wait long.

A new figure stepped on to the stage. A new character in our shadow play, as unmistakeable in silhouette as it was in real life. The globed, flat-topped head was cut at a dramatic angle. And the shadow creature held aloft an umbrella, as if expecting shadow rain.

The goblin shadow was huge and I watched, mesmerised. First, the shadow umbrella closed. They say it's bad luck to have an open umbrella indoors, and I remember wondering – stupidly – whether the goblin might be superstitious. But then it turned that closed umbrella over in its hands, first holding up the hooked handle, then reaching it out towards me.

'*Move!*' shouted Cass, and I knew she was right. But I just stood there, watching.

And then it was all too late.

The handle of the shadow umbrella hooked round my shadow neck. For a moment nothing happened – and then I felt a tug. And in one brutal yank of the umbrella, the goblin pulled my shadow from the wall.

I can't really describe the sensation. If you've ever ripped cloth, you'll know the sound. But the pain was indescribable. As if my skin were being ripped away, but deeper, like I was being torn in half. And my whole body was hot fire as the goblin shadow jumped across, and took the place of my own.

I finally turned then, barely able to breathe from the pain. The goblin was still outside on the terrace, still smiling. It took a step back and gave a little bow – leaning low, contentedly stroking its shadow on the ground. It's *new* shadow. *My* shadow.

'It took my shadow,' I said pointlessly.

Squid looked at me, his face stiff. He was so small now, he literally had to climb down from the armchair. Jumping to reach the ground.

'This has to stop,' he said, looking first to me, then at Cass. He looked half mad, gripping his head with both hands. 'We have to make it stop.' And reaching out, he pushed his hand into the glowing embers of the dying fire. Shouting from the pain, his face rigid, he gave me a final, agonised look – and disappeared.

I looked at Cass. 'We have to go too,' I said simply. Already I could feel my hand getting warm. Squid, awake, back in the library, was making good on his promise to do whatever it took to wake us. I stood there looking at Cass, my palm getting warmer, willing myself to wake before it began to burn.

'No. Not without Dad.'

'But he could be anywhere. We'll never find him,' I said, my hand really starting to burn. It was possibly the most stupid thing I've ever said, because right then, we heard an almighty thump as something smashed on to the floor in the hallway.

We ran out of the library, but I stopped immediately, desperate to find a light switch, patting the wall as Cass ran on.

I'd hardly paid it any attention before, in daylight, but I remembered there was a staircase, spiralling up the far wall. And I could see stars through the big window at the top of the stairs. But the starlight was weak, and the space before me just a black void.

'*Dad?*' Cass's voice was a shriek, but I never had time to wonder why. Because as she screamed, I found the light switch, and with a flick the hall blazed into existence.

'Shut your eyes,' shouted Cass. But it was already too late. I'd seen immediately. The banister at the head of the stairs had been smashed through. And below, on the hard wooden floor, was Cass's dad. His body and legs mangled where he'd fallen, limbs sticking out at strange, unnatural angles. As if his entire body had been shattered by the fall. I saw bone jutting through the front of his shin, and suddenly I was vomiting – right there on the floor.

'You have to unsee this,' shouted Cass. 'Remember your gran's bedroom – we changed it back? Right? You have do that again, now, for my dad. Please, just shut your eyes – and *fix him*.' She looked at me with angry eyes. '*Please*, just do it!'

I shut my eyes, still wiping sick from my face, and tried to think of her dad how he was, lying there in the coffin – before his body and legs were broken. I imagined his face, composed and content, imagined his back straight, his arms healthy.

'It's working,' said Cass. 'Just keep going.'

I tried, I really did, but when my imagination reached his legs – all I could see was that shattered piece of bone, jutting through the skin – blood and marrow oozing on to the floor.

Laughter filled the hall, or maybe just my head, it was impossible to say. And my eyes snapped open – to see a vision straight from hell.

She stood above us, the woman-with-no-eyes, her face obscene, twisted with laughter. Her mouth was wide open with the force of it, showing shattered fragments where teeth should have been, and the little sliced stump of a tongue, as if that too had been cut away in the car accident. Her gurgling laughter was everywhere – a laugh without end.

Cass was immediately running to the stairs, as fearless as she was foolish. She had Betty, the sledgehammer, and she carried it like it weighed nothing – a modern-day

Thor, wielding her hammer of vengeance.

But even as she ran up those stairs, the creature stood immoveable, confident, laughing. And suddenly I knew why. Cass had made a huge mistake. She didn't have the hammer. I could remember it, so clearly, on the floor of the crypt where she'd dropped it.

'Cass!' I shouted a warning. 'You've forgotten – you left Betty in the crypt.'

Cass stopped at the head of the stairs. She turned to me, her face a mixture of horror and disbelief. And the giant hammer, at one moment held high in both hands, was the next ... *gone*.

'Finn, you idiot!' Her face was filled with desperate rage. '*What have you done?*'

'But—' was all I managed. Because I knew. This was a dream. If you want something, you just have to believe it. But like a fool, I'd stopped believing.

The creature never stopped laughing. Not once, not even to breathe. Cass took a step back, suddenly helpless without her hammer. I did the same. Instinctively I stepped backwards, mumbling an apology. Then I slipped and fell, smacking the back of my head on to the hard wooden floor.

I never saw what happened next. Thinking back, I wonder if I was tripped. That's the funny thing about having someone else's shadow: you can never quite trust it. But whatever happened, I smacked down hard – immediately losing consciousness.

After that, everything is a bit jumbled in my head. A few minutes – seconds? – later I opened my eyes to an empty hallway. The lights had gone, but somehow I knew the room was empty.

Lying there on the floor, I could see the broken banister above, and the night sky through the window beyond. My hand was still hot – uncomfortably, burningly hot – and I thought of Squid, awake, back in the library. He'd be getting desperate, but I couldn't wake, not now, not without Cass.

I got to my knees cautiously, then to my feet. My head was throbbing, and my eyes played strange tricks; flashes pulsed across the room like shooting stars. I steadily climbed the stairs, all the while wanting to call out to Cass, but at the same time terrified to make a noise.

There was just one corridor off the landing at the top of the stairs. It ended in a tall, floor-to-ceiling window. Stained glass filled the corridor with shadowy colour, projecting the crude image of a fishing boat and fishermen. It was the sort of window you might see in a church – or I guess an old manor house like this one.

On either side of the corridor though were gun-metal grey doors – each with a square window and bars. The sort you'd only ever see in a prison, or a nightmare.

I stood, uncertain, waiting for a sign.

'Cass?' I whispered eventually.

No reply.

I inched along the corridor, pausing at each door to look inside. The windows were filthy and I had to wipe away thick layers of grime to peer into each room – terrified at what I might find, knowing the creature could spring up from anywhere.

But the rooms were all empty until, perhaps inevitably, I reached the final door at the end of the corridor.

'Cass?' I called out softly, wiping the glass to look inside this final window.

The pain in my hand was getting unbearable. I could literally smell it, like lamb on a kebab. But somehow I pushed away the pain from my mind and cleared a small spyhole in the glass.

Cass stood on the other side of the door, inches away from me. She shouted through the glass.

'*Finn*, you have to get me out of here.' Her eyes were frantic and there was a gash across her forehead. Even through the discoloured glass I could see her face was slick with blood.

I pulled on the bars, but they were solid.

'You can do this, Finn.' Her voice was muffled by the door, but her eyes locked on to mine. 'It's just a dream – believe in yourself.'

I gripped the bars, never once taking my eyes off Cass, and let myself breathe, let myself think. I imagined the bars smaller, thinner and they seemed to shrink in my hands. I literally saw it happen: the metal shrinking down until they were no thicker than spaghetti, then thinner still – strands of wire. I ripped them apart, and without warning, Cass's punch came smashing through the glass, showering me in fragments.

She squeezed my hand and the pain made me cry out.

'The door!' she shouted, pushing down my hands so they gripped on to the metal. 'Pull it, rip it away.'

She stepped back and I pulled, the metal creaking with the strain.

'It's thin,' said Cass, now smiling encouragement. 'Paper thin. Just tear it away.'

And I would have done. I smiled back at Cass as the thick metal shrank. The pain in my hands was fading, and my hands and arms felt impossibly strong. Another moment, and I would have torn everything down.

But something moved in the shadows behind Cass. And I let go of the door.

'What was that?' I shouted, squinting into the gloom.

'Forget it, just focus,' said Cass, struggling to keep her voice steady.

But I couldn't ignore it. Something was moving behind her.

Cass's eyes flashed with anger and tears. 'Come on, Finn. You're special. Why can't you just stop being afraid? *Just once!*'

And then, from out of the gloom behind her, came a face.

That face of a thousand cuts. With bandaged eyes, and red blotches where the blood had soaked through from hollow eye sockets. The creature – I couldn't think of her as a person – seemed to rise up from the floor, a hand grabbing Cass's throat, yanking her head backwards. Pulling her into the shadows.

I reached for Cass through the open window. Our hands locked, and for a moment I thought it would be enough. But Cass's face told me it was hopeless. The grim determination had all gone, leaving nothing but despair.

'If you can't save me,' she said, 'then you have to look away.'

My hand was a burning agony now, but I refused to let go. I shook my head. 'No, we can do this.'

But Cass shook her head, pulling her hand, twisting it free from mine. 'You *must*. Look away,' she said. '*Please*, if you see this, it's fixed. Forever.'

I shook my head again. But even as I did, I knew she was right.

The woman's nails dug into the skin of Cass's throat, gripping on to her windpipe, ready to rip it away. In the eye of my imagination I've wondered a hundred times what happened next.

But I never saw it.

I shut my eyes. Heard Cass cry out in terror. And let tears wash down my face.

16

BACK IN THE LIBRARY

I woke in agony, and to the stink of burning flesh.

Squid's face was over mine, screaming, and I pushed him back with a shout, hurling away the hot coal from my right hand. The skin had started to blister, and all I could think was to chuck Cass's orange juice on it. It didn't look much, but the pain was indescribable.

'Sorry, mate,' said Squid, clutching his own half-cooked hand. 'I tried everything.'

It took me a while to get my wits, but when I did, my first thought was of Cass. Here, out of the dream, she was just lying there – asleep on her mattress. For a moment I thought she might be dead, but I found a pulse in her neck. It was painfully slow.

'Look.' I pointed. There were four livid scratches across her throat. Fingernail marks, but that was all – she was alive. I'd been right to look away when I did.

We tried to wake her, obviously – tried everything, even fire – but it was futile, and we knew it.

'Why didn't you wake *her* first?' I shouted at Squid. *'You could have saved her.'* I wanted to scream at him, wanted to shake him so hard that he'd never forget what he'd done.

But a groan from the study interrupted everything.

After four months locked in sleep paralysis, Cass's dad had woken up – with a wail of anguish.

The rest of the night was a shambles. The injuries to the poor guy's legs were horrific. We called an ambulance right away, but it seemed to take hours to arrive. And all the while we just stood there, listening to his suffering, not knowing what to do, or how to help.

Eventually the paramedics came and took him away. They didn't seem much interested in us and our minor burns and scratches. And we hid Cass well away, in the only place we could think of – her dad's empty coffin.

It was weird putting her in there, and it took both of

us to lift her. I wasn't sure we were doing the right thing, but Squid was certain.

'We need to keep her safe. Her dad's rule, remember? Never force someone awake who's trapped in a dream.'

We got her in, eventually. She lay there, just like her dad had done. Seemingly unharmed and asleep, at peace, barely breathing.

We didn't sleep, obviously, and at about four o'clock, before sunrise, we decided to go back to mine. Anything to get away from Freak House.

Gran was awake when we got home, still sitting on the sofa watching a quiz show. Like she'd forgotten to go to bed.

'Gran?' I didn't want to shock her, so I spoke quietly from the doorway to the sitting room. 'You all right?'

'Quasimodo,' she said, ignoring me.

'Correct,' said the quiz show host.

'Gran?!' I said louder. 'It's time for bed.'

'Porcupine,' said Gran. It was like she couldn't even see me.

'Correct,' said the host.

'Do you think she needs a doctor?' said Squid, looking over my shoulder, but I shook my head.

'It's probably an infection,' he kept on. 'Seriously, it happens to old people all the time. My grandad had

185

a funny turn like that. All he needed was some anti-biotics, and—'

'You'd better go, Squid, you've done everything you can,' I said, not meaning to be unkind. 'Get that hand sorted out before your mum sees it, yeah?'

17

FRIDAY

If ever there was a day to rot in bed, it was Friday.

I didn't even think about going into school, just buried myself under the duvet and hid, from everything. Squid messaged a few times, so I turned off my phone. The home phone rang at about ten, probably school, but I just let it ring. Gran didn't even seem to notice, I could still hear her downstairs in the sitting room, firing answers at the TV.

That's how I spent Friday, with the lights on even in the day, too scared to look at my own shadow. Eventually the sun began to fall, and I had to face my greatest fear of all – sleep. The thought of it made me feel sick. Actually, physically sick. And for a while, I thought I might throw up or go mad, or both. The whole hideous mess of my life just tumbled over and over in my head. Desolation everywhere I looked.

There was just no way out. I was trapped in a living, waking nightmare.

So that's it. Now you know why I'm lying here writing this – to hide from sleep and escape my thoughts. Anything to give my brain a break. I've got one hand in a bucket of water, partly to cool the burned skin, but mainly so I'll wake up if I do accidentally fall asleep. And the other hand's got cramp, from writing this *fear journal* all night long.

You pretty much know everything else too. How, one by one, that woman, that creature, has taken everything from me. *Everyone*. Mum, Dad and now Gran – all gone. Cass is doomed too. And Squid? If I let him try to help, well – he'll be next. There's no escaping this. No escaping that monster.

Believe it or not, I can understand her a bit more now. If she did make her parents disappear, when she was just a little kid, maybe that's enough to turn anybody mad. Maybe that's what's happening to me.

Lying here, terrified to sleep, knowing the harm I might do just by dreaming the wrong thing – knowing the *harm I've already done* – is destroying my sanity. Whatever malicious mix of guilt and fear turned that woman into a monster is doing the same to me.

I think realising this is what decided me. Sure, I could stay here, under the duvet, hiding, going steadily insane with fear and dread. Or I could do something, do anything. Because I don't think anything could ever be worse than this.

Maybe that's why I've decided to go back. It probably sounds like the dumbest idea ever. But if you've read all the way up till here, you'll hopefully understand. I'm tired, *tired all the time*. Yes, from lack of sleep, but it's more than that. I'm tired *of being afraid* all the time. Apart from this last summer, I guess, and those dreams with Cass, I've never known what it's like to live without that heavy, sick sense of dread pressing down on the top of my stomach. It's been there every morning when I wake up, and every night when I go to bed, for as long as I can remember.

I can hear Gran downstairs, still getting the questions right – which is something, I guess. And I think she got something else right too. She's told me the same thing every night for years – but I never really listened. Not till I wrote the words down in this journal: *You've got to face your fears sometime, boy*. That's what she always says. And I see it now. Writing this has made me see just how true it is.

And the 'sometime'? Well, I'm pretty sure, that sometime … is *now*.

The sun will rise in fifteen minutes. They say the darkest hour is just before the dawn. But that's rubbish. I've pulled the curtains and I'm looking at the night sky, right now. I'm looking east and the horizon is already lighter, the black night colouring with shades of blue.

It's time to face my fears, and go back to Freak House.

FRIDAY, 16TH SEPTEMBER

Maybe I shouldn't have been quite so bleak. In the small hours before sunrise, last Saturday morning, it really did look like everything was utterly, totally crap.

Now, a week later, it's time to finish this miserable *fear journal*. Put it to bed, once and for all. Because I can honestly say that facing your fears can literally change *everything*.

I'm not going to lie – it's not that everything will suddenly be peachy. What happened next was truly horrible. But I'll get to all that. The bottom line is that nothing could be worse than that day and night, hiding in my bedroom, paralysed by fear – afraid even to check my own shadow.

So let's go back to Saturday morning, shall we? To the

end of my long day and night of despair. The sun will soon appear at the horizon. There are fifteen minutes until dawn, time for one last dream – one last horror show – that will leave you questioning everything you thought you knew about the universe and our place in it. A nightmare so horrifying, you'll probably never want to sleep again.

I think I'll call it the Freak House Dream.

18

THE FREAK HOUSE DREAM

I lay on my bed, with no real plan in my head. I don't know what I was thinking, really. I'm sure if Cass had been there, she'd have gathered together all sorts of weapons and stuff. Sledgehammers called Betty would have been the least of it. And Squid? He would have had some brilliant, random plan that involved mirrors or lasers or something.

But I had just one thought: *Face your fears*. I was going back to Freak House, to face Cass's dead mum. To face the monster she'd become. To look it in those badly bandaged eyes, and do whatever it took to save Cass.

If that monster wanted her powers back? She could have them. I was done with them. They're nothing but a curse. Or maybe, if I let her destroy me, she'd let Cass go, and leave Squid alone too. That's what I decided as I settled on to my side, ready to sleep.

If you can call that a plan, that was the plan.

The dream started on the long gravel drive leading up to Freak House. Cursing for not dreaming myself closer, I started the long trudge up the driveway.

I'd dreamed a big moon, low on the horizon, and it gave plenty of cold, white light. But even without it there would have been light to see by; the sky was already brightening behind me.

The house looked bigger than before, taller, and I studied it as I walked. The windows that weren't boarded up were black, not a single light shone inside the house. But as I drew closer, I saw movement in one of the upstairs windows. A face looking down. *The* face. Those bandaged eyes might be useless – but she stood looking, nonetheless.

'That's her,' said a voice, and I flinched.

'*Jesus!* Squid? Is that you? You gave me a heart attack. What are you doing here?'

He was hiding in an old wooden barrel by the side of the gravel drive.

'What do you think? I'm waiting for you.'

'In a barrel?'

'It was all I could think of,' he said, looking furtively about. 'I didn't realise how much it would stand out.'

The barrel did look a bit odd, just sitting there on the grass by the side of the path.

'Are you planning on staying in it?'

'No, obviously,' he said, tipping it over and crawling out. 'I was just waiting for you. Have you seen her, at the window? She's been there for ages, it's like she's waiting for us.'

Squid dusted himself down. He was still smaller than real life – but not ridiculously, not like before.

'Squid, you don't have to do this. I can do it on my own. Why don't you just … I dunno, dream yourself to Hawaii or something? I promise, I'll be OK.'

'No can do, matey. You need me.' He looked at me defiantly, still brushing a cobweb off his arm. 'You probably don't even have a plan.'

Now, I could have bluffed it out. I could have sent Squid packing. And right then and there, standing in the moonlight on that long gravel drive, was the exact time to do it. Maybe if I had, Squid would still have all his fingers. But I've always found it hard to say no to Squid. He's got that little toddler smile, remember? It's hard to say no to someone like that.

And besides, Squid's the only real friend I've ever had. Everything always feels better, safer, when Squid's around. Maybe for all of those reasons, I gave him a hug.

'Cheers, buddy,' I said, trying to keep the emotion out of my voice as we sprang apart. 'And you're right, I don't really have a plan. I was just kind of hoping to offer to do anything she wants – in return for Cass.'

'Okaayyy,' he said, unconvinced. 'So your entire plan is to do whatever she wants?'

I nodded.

'I think we can do better. Remember, everything has a weakness. Vampires: garlic. Werewolves: silver bullets. And—'

'That thing?' I interrupted, looking at the face in the window.

'Yes, even that thing.' Squid pulled a small plastic lighter from his pocket, and rolled his finger over the little metal wheel to make a spark.

'Fire. That's the answer. Every mummy horror movie is the same. Mummies with bandages plus fire equals good times.'

'But she's not a mummy – well, not that kind, anyway. She's got one small bandage wrapped round her head.'

'Doesn't matter, she's wearing a hospital gown. I

looked it up. They're polyester – *flammable*. And fire works with zombies too. Look, whatever she is, fire is, like, a universal anti-monster weapon. We just have to get close. Trust me.' He put the lighter back in his pocket. 'Shout when you need it.'

We reached the house quickly after that, painfully aware that our every step was being somehow *sensed* from the window. Gravel crunched loudly as we ran over it, but in some ways it was a relief to be seen and heard. Hiding was no longer an option. And in a night-mare, the hiding is always the worst part.

The black glossy door was already swinging open and I gave it a gentle push, letting moonlight into the big hallway. Cold air blew on to my face, and I remembered Cass's words about how cold it was: *This hallway always gives me the creeps.*

I looked towards the stairs, and Squid nodded. They were wide and shallow – a grand old stairway for a grand old building. They creaked on every step. And by the time we reached the top, I'd had enough of skulking in the shadows.

'Squid,' I said in my normal voice. 'Why are we trying to be stealthy? It's pointless, she knows we're here. And anyway, she *needs* to know we're here. That's the whole plan – we need to get close.'

'So, what are you thinking? You want a torch?' he said uncertainly.

'No,' I said, faking a smile. 'I'm not skulking in the shadows any more.'

I clicked my fingers with more confidence than I actually felt – and the lights came on. *All* the lights.

'Hello, we're here!' I shouted, head raised and with my arms spread wide. 'You can come and say hi if you like.'

The lights began to flicker. But I didn't panic, just focused my thoughts – visualising the dozens of bulbs, imagining them brighter.

And just like that, the flickering stopped.

I smiled at Squid and pulled my shoulders back. 'There, does that feel better?'

He nodded. *'First mover kudos* to us, methinks.'

Facing the back of the house, I shouted again. 'I have what you want,' I said loudly. 'You can have it, all of it. Just give us Cass and it's yours. It's all … yours.'

Curtains blew apart at the window across the landing. The heavy green velvet rippled in a non-existent wind. Then the window started banging, opening and shutting, as if a phantom housekeeper were airing the house.

I focused on the window, saw it fly open, then slam

shut, over and over. The frame looked ready to rattle itself apart, glass shattering on to the wooden floor.

'Make it stop,' said Squid. He put a hand on my shoulder. 'It's OK. You can do this.'

He kept his hand there, on my shoulder, and maybe because of that – or maybe because he sounded so confident – it was suddenly easy. The window slammed shut one last time, and stayed there.

In the silence that followed, I took the chance to breathe.

'What now?' said Squid.

'We find Cass,' I answered, and together we moved steadily to the rear of the house, and that long corridor where I'd last seen her.

It wasn't easy finding our way, even with the lights on. At one point we reached a dead end, with a small narrow staircase leading back down – 'servants' stairs' Squid called them. But eventually we found the small hallway outside the library, and from there it was easy. Climbing the staircase, taking care as we passed the broken banister, we turned into the long corridor.

'Stay where you are.' Cass's voice was clear and strong, and we stopped immediately. She was standing at the end of the corridor – right in front of that ornate stained-glass window. She was staring up at the ceiling.

'Don't move,' she repeated. 'This is some sort of trap.'

'What sort of trap?'

'That sort of trap,' she answered, and we followed her eyes to the ceiling. Squid let out a soft gasp as we saw what was hanging there. Clinging to the light fitting, like a sleeping koala snug on its eucalyptus branch, was the goblin. Its body slowly expanded and shrank with each deep, sleeping breath.

'It's asleep,' said Squid, whispering the obvious.

'But it's got a water pistol,' added Cass. 'One of ours, with holy water.'

'How long have you been trapped here?' I asked Cass, and she shrugged.

'I don't know … it feels like forever.' She suddenly looked confused. 'Or maybe just a few minutes – I don't know. Every time I take a step, it starts to move, and—'

'Cass,' I interrupted. 'Just dream up a frying pan – you know, a skillet.'

'You think I haven't tried?' She looked down at her hand, focused hard … but nothing happened. 'See? Nothing.'

'Hold on,' said Squid behind my shoulder. 'Why are we afraid of holy water? We're the good guys.'

I looked at Cass. 'He's got a point. Why are we scared of holy water?'

Cass opened her mouth to say something sarcastic. At least, that's what it looked like; my best guess was that it was going to be pretty scathing. But then her expression changed.

'You know, you might have a point.'

She inched forward and the goblin started shifting about.

'Clear out the way,' said Cass, waving her hand to make the point. 'I'm going to run, so it doesn't fall on me.'

But it was too late. Like a dead koala falling to the ground, the goblin let go of the light shade and thumped to the floor. We watched in silence as it slowly got to its feet and stretched its limbs. Long arms unfolded themselves, and a big-jointed hand raised the pistol into the air.

Cass looked at Squid, wide-eyed, and whispered, 'What now, genius?'

But Squid never got to make a second genius suggestion. The goblin looked at me with a sleepy smile, then at Cass, before turning the water pistol on itself – squirting into its open mouth.

'It's drinking,' said Squid.

'Don't be stupid,' said Cass, not taking her eyes off the goblin for a second. 'Goblins don't drink holy water.'

It was immediately obvious she was wrong. Squirt after squirt went into its gaping mouth. How it managed to smile throughout I've no idea. But it did. Until, draining the pistol to the last dribble, it turned to me. And gave a bow.

That's when I noticed my shadow on the wooden floor between us, clearly lit by the bulb above – but the angle made it short and stumpy, a mini version of me.

It waved. And somehow I knew it wasn't a wave hello.

It was a wave goodbye.

I looked at the goblin in alarm. It was swelling, like a balloon sculpture – but stretching too far, overfilled with air.

'Guys,' I said worriedly. 'I think something's gonna happen.'

And just like an overpumped balloon dog, the goblin – with a final, forlorn smile – exploded.

The explosion was massive. All this talk of balloons has probably given you the wrong idea. Because the goblin bomb was no popping balloon. It exploded like a grenade – smashing walls and windows, and knocking me and Squid flat on our backs.

With ringing ears, we looked up into a cloud of brick-dust and debris.

'Cass?' I shouted, squinting through the dust. The

window had been blown apart, and we ran to the open gash in the side of the house. Cass had been flung to the ground below.

'Cass!' I yelled. She lay among the rubble of brick and glass, on her back, eyes and mouth wide, looking at the heavens. Like she couldn't believe she was still alive.

And then I saw why: she was clutching her side, holding a large chunk of glass that had somehow lodged in her belly, blood slopping on to the stone slabs beneath her.

'Cass!!' I said, for a third time. 'Don't move.'

But in dreams, you sometimes don't have a choice.

Because suddenly *she* was there. The woman, the creature, who's been torturing my dreams ever since I can remember. Mallory McAllaster – or at least what was left of her broken soul. She stood over her bleeding daughter, looking down at the wound in her belly. For a stupid moment I thought she might be there to help. But then she looked up at us, and the malice and the hatred and the joy on her shattered face was enough to shrivel your heart.

Squid took a step back, but I stood transfixed, watching in horror as she reached down and grabbed the fabric of Cass's top. And, without any effort, began

203

to drag Cass across the grass – the blood from her wound smoothing the way.

Cass screamed, still clutching at the shard of glass stuck in her side. All we could do was stand and stare.

Squid's face was white in the moonlight, and he was shaking uncontrollably. I didn't know what to do either, so I did the first thing that came into my stupefied head: I grabbed him by the back of his hoody – and jumped, smashing through the remnants of glass.

Squid landed badly, all the wind rushing out of him with the force of his fall. But I didn't wait – just ran towards Cass, screaming at the creature as it dragged her through the door to the cemetery.

In a dream you can sometimes run fast – faster than a car, or a bullet, even. But other times your legs pump and you hardly move. Running in slow motion, like you're trying to run through deep sand.

That race across the lawn was agonising. Cass's blood seemed to have churned the soil to sticky mud, and by the time I reached the cemetery, Cass and her mother were gone. Only the open gates of the church crypt suggested where – but it felt like I'd always known where this dream would end. Like I'd always known where everything must end.

I was going into the crypt, for a third and final time.

'Finn!' Squid's shout was breathless, and I waited at the gates of the crypt for him to catch up. 'You need this,' he said simply, handing me a lump of wood.

It was the log I'd thrown at the goblin the night before – still charred black at one end. Squid passed it to me and pulled out his plastic lighter.

'Ready?' he said, his thumb resting on the little wheel.

The torch lit with a whoosh and we both instinctively rocked backwards. It was the sort of thing that could only happen in a dream, but the flame settled quickly and in its yellow light we both nodded, ready to move.

Holding it high, I stepped through the gates and into the crypt. The sight of blood on the stone floor – Cass's blood – drove us onward.

'Cass? Are you there?' I called down into the chamber below, lowering my torch and squinting into the darkness, terrified at what I might see.

Squid was so close behind me I could hear his breathing, like he was right in my ear. Having Squid at my back should have been reassuring, but it just made me feel all the more trapped.

I would have done anything not to go down into that chamber. Absolutely anything to run, and keep running until that creature was a million miles away. I'd have done anything, except for one thing: I couldn't leave Cass to die.

Even so, I never thought I could actually do it. Not really. That's the thing about facing your fears: until you do it, it's just impossible to imagine it will ever actually happen.

In the end, I did it almost without thinking – just put one foot in front of the other. And with my head spinning and my heart squirming, I stepped off that bottom step like I was walking off a cliff. Eyes shut, I thrust the torch forward, like a dagger.

'I knew you'd come.' Her rasping voice echoed round the chamber as soon as I stepped into it. 'Boys will always play the hero. It's so very … pathetic.'

She stood next to the blue light of the open sarcophagus, her back to the wall of coffins, her face full of shadows.

Cass lay on the floor next to her – slumped forward and clutching her side. She looked up at me, squinting like she could hardly focus, her head rocking. She was still alive.

The woman – the creature – sniffed the air. 'You've brought your little, frightened friend too,' she said, with a smile that revealed her shattered teeth.

I held the burning torch towards her; in its light, I could finally take a proper look. At the cuts across her face and neck. The jagged windpipe with its massive, vertical scar. *She must have gone through the windscreen head first*, I remember thinking. *Is that how she'd lost her eyes?* Just the thought churned my stomach.

For the first time I wondered what had happened that morning on the way to work, on 13th June twelve years ago. Did she fall asleep at the wheel? Did someone want her dead? Why wasn't she wearing a seat belt?

She wore a hospital gown, so they must have got her to an emergency room. And her feet were bare, ankles and shins exposed – a dark gash ran along one, the other was mangled and bent. The pain of it must have been unimaginable.

'I'm here to help you.' I spoke for the first time, painfully aware how unconvincing I sounded. 'I can give you whatever you want. I can *do* whatever you want. Please, just let me help her first.' I looked down at Cass, my hands shaking with fear and frustration. 'She's your daughter. Your own flesh and blood.'

The creature turned her head towards Cass, her bandaged eyes unseeing. 'My daughter? She's nothing. Who is she to me? A few donated cells? Some wasted DNA? I have no need of children – I will be *immortal*.'

'But you're already dead,' I said angrily. 'You died twelve years ago. In the name of everything that is holy, just let it go.'

'There is no death for the likes of you and me. Death is just passing through a gateway.' She reached towards the sarcophagus, dipping a hand into its swirling, turquoise light. '*We* can come back. We can always come back. Ask your gran. *She knows.*'

'Then why do you need me?'

'Because seeing is believing. And without these,' she said, touching the bandages that covered her empty eyes, 'it's impossible. Without eyes, my power is a shadow of what it once was. I need your eyes.'

'I understand.' I tried to sound calm. 'You need me to see it? So it comes true. I understand. I can do that. I can help.'

She shook her head, and the muscle of my heart stiffened as I suddenly realised what she really meant.

'No, Finnegan Quick,' she repeated. 'I need *your* eyes. Only you can make me whole again.'

'But … ?' I said dumbly, my thoughts spinning out of control. 'You want my actual eyes? No way. Never in a million years. Is that what all of this has been about?'

The woman's head suddenly kinked to one side, as if she were looking at me for the first time.

'You're right, of course. No one would give up their eyes, not even in a million years. That's why I had to take everything from you first – your dog, your mum, your dad. Your gran protected you, for a while. But soon she'll be gone too. And then what do you have, Finnegan? Nothing. A dismal eternity of lonely fear.'

She moved towards Cass, reaching for the shard of broken glass. Cass tried to twist away, but it was hopeless. The creature grabbed the glass and pulled. New blood spilt even as she raised the weapon, ready to strike another wound.

'So will you do it?' Her voice was an angry croak. Red blood dripped from the glass. And in that moment I knew I didn't have a choice. I just wanted everything to be over.

I nodded, and shut my eyes. I imagined her bandage unwinding, and the empty black sockets beneath, full of congealed, black blood. And then, feeling daggers pricking my own eyes, I imagined hers anew. Blue, just like mine.

'No!' screamed Squid, and he pushed past me. I stumbled, and instinctively opened my eyes. He tried to grab the glass in the creature's hand. But he had to jump to even reach it. It was a stupid, stupid thing to do.

I don't know if you've ever seen someone lose a finger. It's pretty grim. He was lucky only to lose the one, really – it just sliced clean through. Maybe it only does that in a dream – or a cartoon. But Squid's finger, his middle finger, just sliced away at the top joint – spinning into the warm blue light of the sarcophagus.

He landed hard, clutching his hand, staring at his missing fingertip. Blood starting to spurt and he screamed, first at his finger, and then at me.

'Make it stop!' he screamed. *'Just make it all stop!'*

There are points in any nightmare where everything seems hopelessly, irreversibly doomed. Life can sometimes feel like that too. The monster will inevitably look under the bed and discover you. Your teacher will make you stand in class and suddenly everyone will see that you're only wearing underpants. Your friends are wounded, bleeding to death in a miserable, damp underground crypt – and you're doomed to join them. Pretty much all my nightmares reach a point like these. So, in many ways, this nightmare was no exception.

Normally, at that point, I wake screaming into the darkness, just before Gran's rappity-tap-tap on my bedroom door comes to the rescue. But for some reason, Squid's shrieked words did something else. 'Make it stop,' he screamed. 'Just make it all stop.' And, for once, I didn't wake. For once, I did something heroic.

I made everything stop.

The blood from his finger – that's what I noticed first. It was pulsing out in globs one moment, and then the fountain just froze in mid-air. I looked down at Cass; she was frozen too, her face a mask of fury. As if she'd been paralysed midway through calling someone an idiot. My heart raced as I realised what I'd done and, anxious with hope, I looked at the woman-with-no-eyes.

She stood frozen too, her hollow eyes staring, arms still aloft, brandishing the chunk of glass, ready to strike. I touched her shoulder, hardly daring to believe what I'd done. She didn't move.

I'd stopped time.

But for how long? I could feel her vibrating, straining against whatever power was holding her. *My* power, I suddenly thought, with a rising panic.

And then I blinked, only for a second, but I did blink. And in that moment, she moved. With terrible speed, she turned to face me, the glass suddenly angled at my throat. But with my eyes back on her, she was held frozen once more.

I stepped backwards, not taking my eyes off her for a second.

Working quickly, never blinking, never taking my

eyes from the creature, I knelt – and reached out, feeling for Cass on the floor where I'd last seen her.

I used one hand, still holding the burning torch in the other. Such a feeble weapon it seemed now. I found Cass's arm and followed it to the hand – to her fist, which was pressed hard into the open wound of her tummy.

Still looking at the creature, I moved Cass's hand away and pulled aside her torn T-shirt. I couldn't risk a look, so I probed with fingers – feeling the wet, open flesh, willing it to heal. The wound was huge, a gash deep into her belly, bigger than my hand. It must have looked horrific – it certainly felt horrific – and for a moment I feared it would be impossible to heal it without seeing it.

I must have blinked rapidly, distracted by my thoughts, imagining Cass's sliced skin fusing together – the blood vessels beneath rejoining and healing. It took only a moment, but the woman – the creature – had moved again: she now stood bending over me, frozen once more, but with the glass shard pressing hard against the side of my neck.

I scrambled backwards, still on the floor, and didn't take my eyes off her for a nanosecond. Shuffling towards Squid, always keeping my eyes on the creature, I felt for his arm and then his finger. It was sticky, gooey, and it was all I could do not to look at it.

I fixed Squid's finger like that – sitting there, staring at that creature, at her face. I never took my eyes off her. Maybe that's why Squid's finger never properly healed.

After that I managed to get to my feet. My eyes were sore, scratchy and painful, but I refused to blink – knowing one blink might be my last.

Every instinct was screaming at me to run. It's what I'd been doing for years. And it worked, it kept me safe. But Gran's words kept repeating in my head: *Face your fears*. There's something else she sometimes says too, a famous quotation. You've probably heard it as well: 'Cowards die many times before their deaths. The valiant never taste of death but once.'

I looked at the creature, frozen in time – her face contorted in rage, her weapon thrust forwards. I walked around her, saw her from every angle, and decided I'd died enough times. Enough times to last a lifetime. And I was ready to stop.

The sarcophagus glowed its welcome, but I no longer yearned for it. Instead, it offered a different chance of escape. Because once this creature had passed through, I realised, I could start living.

After that it was almost simple. I pushed her, lifting her gently over the stone rim of the sarcophagus. She tipped, and fell, embraced by the light.

And was gone.

Squid put his hand on my shoulder, time and movement restored. He pulled me backwards, and at first I didn't understand why.

But then I saw Betty, swinging through her violent arc of demolition. And Cass, with a stony face but glistening eyes, smashed the sarcophagus to a hundred pieces of rubble.

AFTERMATH

After something like that, you'd think the sheer relief would make everything just be wonderful.

But reality doesn't work like that. Take away one thing to worry about and something else rears up in its place. Besides, it's not like all my problems suddenly went away. Mum and Dad were still gone. And Gran, well, she's still not completely back to her old self, even after the antibiotics. Squid was half right – the doctor gave her penicillin for some sort of infection – and it really made a difference. She's still forgetful, but at least she's stopped watching TV all the time. Three days solid, she sat on that sofa. But I knew we were going to be OK when she got her sense of humour back. The last time the doctor came she totally freaked him out by pretending to be dead.

Cass's dad came out of hospital today too – and I went back to the house, Freak House. Maybe that's why I'm writing this, finishing the story, because he had a lot to say. And he also had questions. Questions I'm not sure I know how to answer. But I'll get to all that.

He's in a wheelchair, because of his legs. The doctors think he might be like that forever because the bones in his ankles were shattered, literally shattered, when he fell. But he seems, like, totally OK with it – just happy to be out of hospital and 100 per cent focused on all the things he *can* do. Which is amazing.

Anyhow, we had drinks in the garden, on the terrace, the four of us. Squid was there too. And believe it or not, it's really lovely there in the day – the perfect English country garden. Cass even got out an old croquet set, and between jugs of her home-made lemonade (I know: unbelievable, right?), Squid taught us how to play.

Meanwhile, Cass's dad – or 'Prof', as Squid insisted on calling him – answered my questions. He looked younger out of the coffin (who wouldn't?) and bigger; his broad shoulders and thick arms shunted his wheelchair around with speed. When he spoke, his American accent was strong, much stronger than Cass's – a hangover from growing up in Nashville, 'where the music comes from', as he explained. Anyhow, he had lot to say. Probably best if I just tell you what I can remember.

'She wasn't always a monster, you know,' he said, backing his chair into some shade.

'Cass said her mum changed – after she died?'

He laughed at that, a flat, empty laugh. 'You could say that, but she started changing even before that. When I first met her, Mallory was this huge bundle of brilliant energy – she had so many ideas and plans. But over time she became more and more strung out. She just became obsessed with her dreams.'

The Prof jabbed at his ice with a straw, and we both watched lemonade bubbles fizz to the surface. 'By the end,' he continued, 'Mallory's dream powers were so strong, she was so good at controlling her dreams that she could do almost anything. Money, power, fame – everything. But with her it came at a terrible cost.'

'What do you mean?'

'Her sleep – she had to restrict herself to twenty minutes. Any more and things could get … out of control.'

I nodded. I knew the feeling. My longest, deepest sleeps were always the worst. The dreams could spiral off anywhere.

'Trouble was, the one thing she really, truly wanted … was always out of reach.'

'What was it?' I asked, suddenly nervous to hear the answer.

'She wanted her parents back. That was her obsession, if you like.'

He took a moment to pick something out of his drink before continuing. 'She dreamed them away, you see. When she was just a little kid. God knows what happened, but she was angry and she dreamed them out of existence. For that, she never forgave herself. Her whole life was one desperate attempt to bring them back. To make amends.'

The sweat started to prick through the skin of my scalp, and suddenly I couldn't swallow. I put down my glass, struggling to control my breathing.

'But I did the same,' I said. 'Exactly the same. I dreamed my parents away too.'

'No.' He shook his head violently. 'Never think that. What Mallory did to her mom and dad was done out of anger and hate. What happened to your parents was not your fault. *None of this* is your fault.'

'But does that even matter? You talk about *dream powers* as if it's a good thing, but it's not – it's a curse. And maybe I'm cursed to become a monster, just like her?'

'*No*, there's no such thing as destiny, only probability. What I'm saying is you gotta be careful. Real careful.

Sleep right – no matter what. And don't use your power unless you *absolutely have to*. Above all, we gotta do everything we can to bring back your mom and dad.' He looked right at me, his serious, black eyes reminded me of Cass. 'Me and Cassie, we'll do everything we can to help.'

'But how?' I said loudly. 'They're dead.'

The others were still busy playing croquet but they both looked up. The Prof took the chance to call them back to the table.

'I have a suggestion. A proposal,' he said, when Cass and Squid had finally settled into their chairs. 'That we, all of us, work together to find Finn's parents.'

'But … they're dead,' said Squid. 'I mean, they passed on, through the gateway. There's no coming back from death.'

'What if there were?' the Prof replied to Squid, but he was looking at me. His words hung in the air, filling the silence. After a long pause he continued. 'What if I told you that I know *for a fact* that there's a way back? That gateways can work *both ways*?'

'But we destroyed it,' said Cass. 'It's not even there any more.'

The Prof hadn't seen the state in which we'd left that sarcophagus, and after a faint stirring of hope, I felt another door slam shut.

'She's right,' said Squid. 'Betty smashed it to bits.'

'But that's just one gateway.' The Prof had a sparkle in his eyes. 'There are plenty more. Hundreds, thousands – all over the world.'

'But how do we find them?' I said. 'They could be absolutely anywhere.'

He laughed then, leaning forward on to the table with his big Tennessee smile glinting in the sun. 'That's my job. Wherever there's a true paranormal event, I'll show you a gateway. Trust me, I've been doing this half my life, and there's *always* a gateway.'

'What about all the *fake* paranormal events?' Squid piped up. 'You know, all the made-up stuff. And not just lies. People imagine all sorts of crazy things – most of the stuff on the internet's not real.' Squid looked at me. 'Do you remember that weeping angel statue that turned out to be a leaky roof? Mum's got a book at home called *Explaining the Unexplained*. It's full of stories like that one. Most of the time it's just a scam.'

'That's why you need me,' said Cass's dad, still smiling. He looked suddenly younger, like the thought of sifting through a thousand wacko stories had given him a bolt of energy. 'I've spent half my life studying this stuff. It's my job – sifting wheat from chaff.'

I looked at Cass, but her face gave nothing away.

'Look,' said the Prof, pulling out his phone. 'I saw this yesterday.' He thumbed around and then turned his phone so we could all see. 'Neat little story, I can pretty much guarantee it's not a fake.'

Cass took the phone. 'This isn't English,' she said.

'Hit translate,' said her dad, reaching over.

An icon whirred for a bit, and then the news headline popped back on to the screen. In awkward English.

'*Something is eating the lions,*' read Squid, as Cass scrolled down. '*The Mayor of Brasov today shut the town's municipal zoo because another lion carcass had been discovered within the zoo compound. The cat had been …*' Squid stopped reading and looked up with a grimace. 'Oh, that's disgusting.'

'It's probably just other lions,' said Cass, studying the photographs. 'Too little space, probably, so they turned on each other.'

'Nope. Look at the photos.' The Prof was squinting, the sun now on his face. 'No signs of fighting, just a single killing blow. A blow that left a three-hundred-pound pride male completely eviscerated. Even a tiger couldn't do that.'

Cass and Squid seemed mesmerised by the endless photographs, but I couldn't help feeling they'd missed the point.

'Are you really saying that if we investigate enough weird stuff like this … that sooner or later we'll find another gateway?'

The Prof smiled, even as he noisily sucked at the ice cubes in the bottom of his glass. 'I guarantee it. I've found dozens, over the years.'

We sat there looking at each other, each of us nursing, I'm sure, very different thoughts. At that point I only really had one question.

'You said earlier that you know *for a fact* that gateways can work both ways.'

The Prof nodded, then wheeled himself away from the table. 'Follow me,' he said, moving on to the lawn. 'There's something you really need to see.'

We had to help him once we reached the cemetery. The graveyard had odd slopes and mounds where the earth had shifted over the years. But eventually we reached the gravestone he was looking for.

'You probably don't remember this,' he said, the smile gone. 'I tried to show you once, in a dream. But you didn't want to see it.'

I followed his gaze to the gold lettering. It stood out clearly against the black granite. And despite every instinct telling me not to, I read the words out loud.

'Rosalind "Rose" Quick. Beloved Mother to Christopher. Rest in Peace. Born 12th April 1951, Died—'

'Isn't that your gran's name?' Squid interrupted before I could finish.

I looked at him and nodded. 'And Christopher's my dad's name.'

'But that's not possible,' said Squid, looking at the stone. 'That would mean she died a year before you were even born.'

I turned to Cass's dad, my eyes demanding answers.

'Not impossible, Finn. I told you. Some people come back. The gateways, sometimes they work the other way.'

'So my gran is ... dead?' I spoke slowly, barely able to form the words. 'Or is she alive?'

'Maybe she's both. Who knows, maybe we all are. But she was certainly dead once. I checked the records. Your gran – the woman you've been living with for all these years – died before you were born.'

We stood there in silence, all of us. Lost in our thoughts. Eventually Squid spoke. He'd come to the same conclusion I had.

'Well, I don't know about anyone else,' he said. 'But I'm in.'

A new nightmare.

A deadly premonition.

Prepare for Finnegan Quick's
next investigation.

THE FATE OF
FINNEGAN
QUICK

COMING SOON

Turn the page for a sneak
peak ... if you dare.

THURSDAY, 27TH OCTOBER

My name is Finnegan Quick, and I am exceptional. But not in a good way.

In fact, I'm exceptional in a really, quite astoundingly crappy way. My life is a total mess. And it's all because of the nightmares.

You know how if you wet yourself in a dream, you wet yourself in real life? Well, my dreams are a bit like that. I don't wet myself – *obviously*. What I mean is, everything that happens in my dreams can change real life. Dream a bruise? I can wake up with a bruise. Lose an eye? Yep, gone. My best mate, Squid, lost the top of his middle finger. You can even lose stuff you wouldn't think you could lose – I've lost my shadow, my actual shadow.

Now, you're probably thinking I should stop whining and dream myself up a Ferrari or a yacht or whatever. But it never seems to work out like that. It's always the bad stuff that comes true. The really bad stuff. I lost my mum and dad when I was just a little kid. And my dog. One night I just dreamed they were taken away, and *PAFF*, the next morning they were gone. Forever.

I'd be totally alone right now, or in an orphanage or something. Except somehow, I managed to dream my gran back from the dead. So that's my family: me, an undead gran and nobody else. Not even a goldfish. It's just too risky.

Lucky for me, I've got mates: Squid and Cass. And together with Cass's dad (who is – very usefully – a billionaire) they're helping me find my parents. Because if I can bring Gran back from the dead, well, anything is possible, right?

It's a long shot, and to succeed we need *a portal* – a route to the afterlife so we can go and bring them back. We already found one portal, but then accidentally managed to smash it to pieces. So that's why we set up as paranormal detectives, to find another one. Because wherever there's creepy, supernatural, weirdo stuff happening, there's usually a portal.

You still following me? If you've got a problem, no

matter how weird it is – then the *Freak House Investigators* can help. Maybe your baby sister's a warlock and nobody believes you, or perhaps your teacher's growing hair in unusual places around the full moon. We'll investigate absolutely anything; our first case was a dead gerbil leaving messages on the bathroom mirror. But that turned out to be just a prank.

Unfortunately, or maybe fortunately, most things are fakes. People make up all sorts of guff if it means they get to be famous for fifteen minutes.

But our latest case looks totally legit. Squid found it on the internet. We call it 'The Case of the Teenage Daisy-Chain Death Banshee'.

Or just 'The Banshee Case', for short.

Here are the basics:

Twelve years ago, a teenage girl died in Ballynabas, a little fishing village on the west coast of Ireland. Except she didn't die. At least, not completely.

It's the custom there to lay out the body in an open coffin on the dining room table – so that relatives and friends can come to say goodbye. Weird, I know. But it's what they do. And in the days leading up to the funeral, a strange secret emerged.

Because the body of the girl stayed perfect. Lips plump, cheeks rosy – even her hair kept growing. And the smile on her face? Never faded once.

But there was something else, something even creepier.

When she died, the girl was holding a chain of flowers, daisies. Each day the daisies would wilt, and then die. But each morning she'd be holding a new chain, like it was freshly picked.

You can imagine, by the day of the funeral the villagers spoke of not a lot else. And when her mum refused to have her buried, the talk turned dark.

For months she lay there in that coffin, not dying – every morning a fresh daisy chain in her hands. Other extraordinary things began to happen. People said that her eyes would sometimes open, that she'd watch you, in total silence. And after that, well, things got really weird.

Some nights a shrieking was heard coming from the house. Like the 'wail of a *Banshee*' they described it. And sure enough, like all Banshee screams, the wail predicted death.

Sheep were found in the local fields, their throats ripped open. People in the village started getting sick, some even died. And so when the ancient spring that fed the local spa hotel ran dry, it was the final straw.

Everyone went nuts. Bricks were chucked through windows, threats were made. And the girl's mum was forced to move away – taking her daughter to a deserted island just off the coast.

According to Squid's research, they still live there, in an old, abandoned lighthouse. The mother comes to shore in a rowboat once a week for food and supplies. The villagers still talk, but only after dark when doors are safely locked. Because the Banshee of Ballynabas is never far from anyone's thoughts.

They say the body of the girl never changed. Even as the years went by she stayed a girl, the smile not fading, fresh daisies each morning. But how 'they' know that is anyone's guess. At first, I thought it was just some stupid ghost story too. Something for scaring the kids at Halloween.

But it's not. It's all true.

I know because I, Finnegan Quick, have been inside that old lighthouse.

I've seen the dead girl.

And she's seen me.

1

THE LIGHTHOUSE DREAM

It was a disaster right from the start.

The first mistake was leaving Cass behind. Cass is the sort of person who can kick a Banshee in the head without even warming up her hamstrings. She's exactly who you want by your side in the middle of a nightmare. But as she pointed out: 'Only a numbskull with a death wish would go anywhere near a Banshee.'

The second mistake was bringing Squid, but he insisted.

He may be my best mate, and he may be a total genius when it comes to knowing stuff. But when it comes to taking on a Banshee in an abandoned lighthouse on a remote Irish island covered in sheep – he's worse than useless. Literally, worse than useless. For a start, he's scared of sheep.

'They're everywhere,' Squid whispered harshly. His eyes were big, shining in the moonlight.

'So?'

We'd dreamed ourselves onto the island's little beach. That's how we do most of our investigating – using dream tech. Which basically means you get hi-resolution satellite images of where you want to go, and then dream yourself there. Sounds complicated and slightly impossible, but it's not. Not once you practice.

Except this time we got the co-ordinates a bit off and were lucky not to end up in the Atlantic. The sheep were shuffling across the sand towards us and Squid had backed away. Another couple of steps and he'd be in the sea.

You couldn't really see the sheep, just their eyes. They were black, the sheep and the eyes – everything was black. Which was weird. An island of black sheep with black eyes. The thought made me pause.

'Look at them,' said Squid. 'They're trying to surround us. *No, don't look at them* – don't make eye contact. The alpha will take it as a challenge.'

'Just keep moving,' I hissed. The sheep *were* getting close, but he was being ridiculous. 'We're here to investigate a Banshee. Not pick a fight with a herd of sheep.'

I took a step forwards, Squid's little body pressed into my back.

'Sheep *kill*.'

'You're thinking of cows,'

'No, sheep. I watch the news, remember. They *trample*.' He mouthed the word like it might give the sheep ideas if they heard it.

I shook my head, but couldn't help but notice the black eyes moving closer. I edged forwards, nervous for the first time.

'And they can smell fear.' He just wouldn't stop. 'Make yourself look big.'

But before I could do anything, the sheep parted, making us a passage off the beach. I ran through it and up on to the stone steps, not stopping till I'd reached halfway to the lighthouse.

The steps had been cut into the rock and we knew from the satellite images that they curved a path up to the lighthouse door. The building itself was small – not much taller than two houses stacked on top of each other. But looking up the hill of steps at it now, inside the dream, the lighthouse seemed massive.

Its wide silhouette cast a heavy shadow in the moonlight, and an eery glow shone from inside – feeble electric lights, or maybe an oil lamp. As we got closer to the lighthouse door, the thrum of a diesel generator gave us the answer. Electric.

'Is that a generator?' said Squid.

'I guess so,' I said, my hand on the iron handle of the big, wooden door. But Squid's hand on my shoulder made me stop.

'You remember the Banshee Rules?' he said quietly.

'Yep, I remember,' I said. 'Now come on, we don't have long.'

Our investigation protocol is to limit dreams to five minutes max. Much more than that and things usually go a bit haywire.

But Squid's hand didn't budge. 'Rule 1: Don't wake a sleeping Banshee.'

'I told you – I remember.' I spoke as loudly as I dared.

'Rule 2,' he continued. 'Don't look it in the eye. That's how it sees your future.'

I turned back towards him with a sigh. Sometimes you just have to let Squid talk.

'If a Banshee looks at you, then you won't be able to move, and if it screams,' he continued, 'then they've *seen your death*. There's nothing you can do. It's worse than voodoo. No matter how fast or far you run, no matter where you hide – Death will *get* you.'

'Ok, I get it. Can we just—'

'Rule 3,' he finished. 'If it touches you, give up. You're already dead.'

'Look, we're just gonna check it out – no wakey Banshee, no looky, no touchy. OK? I just want to find out if this thing is real. Then we get out.'

'Quick,' he added. 'Then we get out … *quick*.'

'Sure,' I nodded with a smile. 'Quick is almost my middle name. Ready?'

But before I could take a step, the hum of the generator suddenly stopped, and the gentle light from within disappeared.

'*It knows we're here*,' whispered Squid in a voice loud enough to wake a Banshee.

'Probably because you won't shut up,' I whispered back.

'So what do we do now?'

'We're the Freak House Investigators, what do you think we do? We go freakin' investigate.'

And, turning away, I opened the big wooden door and stepped inside.

Which, thinking back, was probably my third mistake.

Now, given everything I've said about how my dreams are different – about the bruises, and losing eyes and fingers and even my own shadow – you're probably wondering how we could be stupid enough to dream ourselves into an old, Banshee-haunted lighthouse.

And you've got a point.

But the bottom line is, we set up the Freak House Investigators because it's the only way I'm ever going to find my mum and dad. I *need* to do this. But it doesn't make it any easier. And I can honestly say, hand on heart, as I stepped through the door into that creepy old lighthouse, that I was crapping myself.

It smelled – the lighthouse I mean. That was the first thing I noticed. Most people can't smell in dreams, but I can. I want to say something dramatic, like, 'It smelled of death.' But it didn't – it was more like old fish fingers and peas.

Inside was so dark we could hardly see, at least at first. But we didn't really need to. Squid had somehow found the lighthouse plans online, and we'd memorised everything.

The lighthouse building was circular, with a massive iron pillar that ran upwards through its middle. Two doors led off from the main entrance room. A trapdoor in the floor went down into a basement. We weren't going anywhere near the basement – we're not totally stupid. The other door, a normal door, led straight on to some stairs, spiralling their way right to the lantern room at the top.

The door opened with the smallest of creaks. And even stepping on to the wood and iron staircase, we barely made a sound. Which was a bonus. Squid was right behind me as we moved up through the three floors. First, we emerged up into a giant kitchen – with an old, cold iron stove and a big table built around the central iron pillar. Nobody home.

We took another turn of the spiral staircase and came up into some sort of living room. With old sofas and overflowing bookshelves that ran in a giant semi-circle halfway round the room.

'Still no Banshee,' said Squid ominously.

I looked at the ceiling. Somehow I'd known we'd have to go right to the top. But when I turned back, Squid's head was shaking, words struggling to come out of his open mouth.

'Mate,' I put my hand on his shoulder, 'it's OK. Honestly, you go back, I'll just be a minute. Have you got your peg?'

We have clothes pegs for situations like this. A peg on the top lip is painful enough to wake you up, without causing any lasting damage. Sounds obvious, but believe me, It took a lot of trial and error before we came up with that. I've got the scars to prove it.

Squid shook his head.

'No,' he said firmly. 'We do this together. Banshee Rule 4: Never face a Banshee alone.'

I didn't deserve Squid. I thought about saying something, but I knew it would come out all garbled and embarrassing. So I just nodded, and tried to smile.

We took the final turn of the staircase. Still not even a creak. And I inched my head into the lantern room – the room that held the lighthouse beacon. The ceiling steepled up into darkness, but the walls were pure glass and starlight filled the room.

The beacon at the centre looked like a hulking alien head. Prisms of glass were wired on to a metal frame in the shape of a space helmet, or maybe one of those old diving helmets, but massive. Two circles of glass faced us like giant eyes, and for a moment I couldn't stop staring back.

Squid tugged on my arm, and nodded towards the far side of the room.

Laid out on a low bed, or couch, was a girl. *The* girl.

She was clutching a string of daisies, peaceful, asleep, maybe dead. But maybe not.

She certainly looked dead. In the cold starlight her

skin was bone-white, like all the blood had been drained from her veins.

Moving slowly, we crept up into the room, and I reached for the little mirror in my back pocket. It's an old doctors' trick from the days of plagues. You didn't want to touch a dead body if it might give you Deathpox, so you couldn't check for a pulse with your hand. But if the mirror fogged up, then you knew the person was still breathing.

The mirror was Squid's idea, obviously. He reads history books too. But even more obviously, I was the one to actually do it. There was no way I'd let Squid get that close to a Banshee.

He put his hand on my shoulder, and for a bad moment I thought he was going to start talking Banshee Rules again. But he just gave me a good-luck squeeze.

I walked softly, kung fu-style, keeping to the edge of the circular room. The walls were all glass, a giant circular window, and the view was astonishing. An endless ocean, thick black but dotted with swells of white surf.

I expected the old wooden floor to betray me at any moment, but I was lucky, and worked my way round the room silently, now focused entirely on the girl. She wore a long, white dress and had been laid on her back, arms across her chest – like a sleeping Dracula, except with flowers and prettier hair. She was pretty too, but in a bloodless, possible-vampire way. Even so, I couldn't take my eyes off her face. Dead or alive she was beautiful, totally at peace, with just the hint of a smile. Like the legend had said, as if she were having the happiest of dreams.

That's when Squid farted.

It wasn't totally unexpected. According to Squid, he holds 'a lot of his stress in his digestive tract'. But it wasn't the best timing. To be fair, it was the faintest of farts. More of a bat-squeak than anything major. So quiet we'd have probably gotten away with it. But Squid's mum has always brought him up with proper manners.

'Pardon me,' he said, forgetting to whisper. And we were instantly doomed.

The girl's eyes flicked open.

Her face didn't move, didn't even twitch, but the eyelids lifted and her eyeballs started moving – searching the room – searching for *us*.

We'd broken Banshee Rule 1.

And a moment later, her nearest eye settled on me. I just stood there, staring back – like I'd never even heard of Banshee Rule 2.

And then she sat up, and turned towards me. She seemed to float up off the couch and on to her feet. I couldn't move.

I like to think I'm pretty good in a dream crisis. After all, I've had plenty of practice. But this? I've never felt anything like it. She just fixed me with her green eyes and the blood and colour seemed to surge back into her face – like an artist was painting her as I watched. Freckles dotted her skin, lips and cheeks pinked, and her hair seemed to burn copper-red in the moonlight. She was immediately very alive.

She came towards me. At least I think she did, because suddenly she was there, right in my face, so close I could smell her – fresh as meadow flowers. She smiled, but there were no vampire teeth, just the hint of braces. It was a victory smile, like she'd just won a race, or a game. 'Kiss chase,' I remember thinking, suddenly aware how close her lips were to mine.

'Finnegan Quick, I knew you'd come,' she smiled again, the braces glinting. 'You have to understand, *it's a soul for a soul.*'

I didn't know what to say to that. But I didn't have long to not say it, because as she stared at me, only inches away, her face changed.

The smile vanished, and her eyes widened – first in

horror and then disgust, as she gazed into my eyes. And then, before I could even think to move, she was screaming. Screaming with all the force of her lungs. So loud I thought she'd burst my ears, so loud I couldn't even think. She screamed in *revulsion*, because staring into my eyes, she'd somehow seen my future.

Maybe I started screaming then too, I'm not really sure. Because suddenly I was in another dream – a dream within a dream – or maybe a vision …

I stood on the bank of a little lake. It was night-time, but the moon was massive – its reflection warm on the black water. There was a cave on the other side, and shadows outside – they were moving, fighting.

For a moment I thought I'd get to see them, but then a cloud must have passed over the moon because everything darkened. One of the figures raised some sort weapon, but I couldn't see what.

Time seemed to slow down, or maybe speed up – and the lake flowed towards me, carrying a shape in the water. It snagged itself against an overhanging tree, and I saw it clearly for the first time. A body, face down in the water.

Even from behind, it was unmistakeable. Squid – in his favourite jeans, and the purple hoody he always wears.

The scream of the banshee filled everything – the air, the water, the earth, everything. It filled my chest, until I was screaming too.

Then I was back in the lighthouse, the Banshee even closer – almost touching me, her eyes locked on mine. She'd stopped screaming, but tears ran down her face; her hand reached up to touch mine. And despite the sheer horror of everything, I couldn't help but think again, how beautiful she was.

I could still see the vision reflected in her eyes – the lake and the cave and the shadowy figures fighting on the far shore. The light grew brighter, burning away the shadows as if the moon was escaping from behind the clouds. And I knew that in another moment, the shadowy figures would be revealed.

'Orla??'

A shout came from somewhere below. A woman's voice. Angry.

'*Orla!*' the voice shouted again.

I should probably have had a thousand thoughts, but the girl's hand was almost touching my face – and I only really had one: Squid's gonna kill me when he finds out I've broken Banshee Rule 3.

But Squid had other ideas. He slammed into me,

flying out of nowhere, smashing into my side like a mini wrecking ball. I let out a grunt as he knocked all the wind out of me, and together we went crashing through the nearest window, glass exploding.

For all the use it did, we clung to each other as we fell, the sea below lurching towards us with horrifying speed. Knowing my luck, we'd have probably missed the massive ocean and smacked right on to one of the little jagged rocks.

But I woke up long before we got anywhere near them.

ABOUT THE AUTHOR

Larry Hayes is afraid of zombies in lifts, vampires in rocking chairs and baby crocodiles in toilets. He is no longer afraid of the dark, changing a nappy in a moving vehicle, or death. He is the author of the How to Survive series, the latest of which, *How to Survive Time Travel*, was shortlisted for the Laugh Out Loud Awards. When he's not writing children's books, Larry works in finance, helps run a homeless charity and is the governor of a primary school federation.